Richard Mace

The First Families

A tale of North and South

Richard Mace

The First Families
A tale of North and South

ISBN/EAN: 9783337000196

Printed in Europe, USA, Canada, Australia, Japan

Cover: Foto ©Andreas Hilbeck / pixelio.de

More available books at **www.hansebooks.com**

The retail price of this book is twenty five cents. This is the price at which it should be bought from booksellers; the price at which it can be bought direct from the publisher.

FRANK A. MUNSEY.

THE FIRST FAMILIES

A TALE OF NORTH AND SOUTH

BY

RICHARD MACE

NEW YORK
FRANK A. MUNSEY
1897

THE FIRST FAMILIES.

I.

A TINY little apartment on a cross street in New York, not too far from the "Tenderloin District." There is a *degage* air about the little parlor which is extremely fascinating to the man who likes a cigar after dinner, and to put his feet on something. There are ottomans and cushions, endless cushions covered with bright striped stuffs that look as though tired heads knew them.

The piano is open, and so is the writing desk. There is music on one, and scattered leaves on the other. By the one table sit the husband and wife, whose gatherings of fluff have gone to create this nest: Mr. and Mrs. Baylor.

" Two hundred and eighty, and six hundred and forty, certainly make—let me see. Yes!

They certainly do make nine hundred and twenty. The Lord only knows where it is, but we are some better off than we ought to be."

"Count your money," says Mrs. Baylor, with the inspiration of a bright idea.

Mr. Baylor goes down into his pockets, and comes up with a little leather purse, which is evidently the sole receptacle of his worldly wealth, for after he discovers it, he goes no farther in his process of exploration.

He takes out three or four untidy wads, which spread out into bank notes. There are also in the purse two blue coupons torn from theater tickets, a key, and a crumpled card, all of which he empties out.

"Dear me!" Mary says, taking up the bits of pasteboard. "Here are our coupons for last night. *Wasn't* Ada Rehan the loveliest creature you *ever* saw? That voice of hers is just music."

"She wouldn't be anything if it were not for Daly. He *forces* her. She'd be playing——"

There was an angry flush upon Mrs. Baylor's face, but her voice was calm and entirely free from expression.

"I suppose you think she ought to have gone on the stage from upper Fifth Avenue, to be able to play in the parts she plays at Daly's?"

"Well, not *much!*" says Mr. Baylor with emphasis, still engaged in unfolding and trying to decipher the card he has taken out. He wonders what in the deuce it is, and how he ever happened to put it there.

There is mollification at once on the very brilliantly colored and mobile face of Mrs. Baylor, and she turns her attention again to the hat she is trimming. Both of them seem to have forgotten the little pile of money on the table.

"This card! Why, this card is that address at Atlantic City—that little house where Janeway was last year, when he went to write up that story about the Middletons. We meant to go down there this spring for a while, but I suppose your everlasting anxiety

to go down to Ellenbro' and live in a house
of your own will knock us out of all that."
Mr. Baylor lighted a cigarette and puffed at it
with the true spirit of the dilettante. "I only
hope, my dear Polly, that you'll like it when
you get there."

"*Like* it? Of course I'll like it," says Mrs.
Baylor with conviction. "Who wouldn't like
it? Aren't we going to live in our own big
house, with room to turn round in, and isn't
Dolly going to have a pony, and I a garden?
And aren't we going to have money enough
so that you can write your great play in peace
and comfort, *and*——" Mrs. Baylor's voice
ended in a gasp of satisfaction.

"We can go abroad on that money," says
Mr. Baylor, "and live about in all the places we
have dreamed of. We can go down to Al-
giers, to Florence, to Nice, to Monte Carlo.
You can live very cheaply over there. Three
thousand dollars a year isn't much to keep up
a big old place like Castle Hill, but it is
riches to us if we keep on living as we've been
doing."

"That's exactly what I'm just not going to do. It's all very well for you and me, but *Dolly* is going to be brought up a *lady!*"

Mr. Baylor winced just the least trifle.

"I hope she'd be that wherever she was brought up—like her mother before her," he said with courtesy.

"You know what I mean, Dick, just as well as I know myself. I want Dolly to *always* have things like other girls. I want her to have a home, not to be knocked about from pillar to post, and friends—and *you* know."

Mr. Baylor was of the blond type, considerably older than his wife and rather *blasé*. He hated with a hatred that passeth understanding, anything sentimental or disagreeable. Now he went back to his wads of money and his card.

"There's forty dollars here. According to that account, I ought to have ninety. I'm blessed if I know what's become of the rest of it."

"What's the difference?" says Mrs. Baylor

with serenity. "What difference does money make to us *now?* We're *rich!*"

A shrill whistle comes up from the street, and there is a sharp, short ring at the flat bell. Mrs. Baylor puts her pretty head out of the window.

"It's the postman," she announces, and having delivered herself of this superfluous piece of information, she goes calmly back to the mirror and devotes herself to trying the effect of various eccentric bends in the brim of the new hat.

"*Isn't* it a beauty?" says Mrs. Baylor, with justifiable pride. "When it comes to hats, it takes an artist's touch. For my part, I pity the woman whose only resource is a milliner's shop. Poor witless things!"

Mrs. Baylor has been married four years, but her cheeks are as rosy and her eyes as happy and gay, and her movements as free as though she were sixteen and just out of a gymnasium. She had never been of sufficient consequence to have her beauty questioned. Most of the people she knows are men, men who are her husband's friends and hers, and they have frankly admired her; told her when her clothes were becoming, and criticised them when they were not. But it would be an ugly garment and a very critical man that must come together to find Mary Baylor anything but sweet and charming and delightful. The sweetness of springtime is in her breath, and the sunny heart of summer in her smile.

Baylor thinks all this as he looks at her, posing before him, light footed, the hat she has just made set jauntily on her head.

"Mary, my darling," he says calmly, as one stating a judicial fact, "you'll simply *loathe* it down in Ellenbro'."

"Not I," says Mrs. Baylor.

There is a quick staccato knock at the door, and almost before it can be answered there is a good humored, foreign looking face, the face of a man of sixty, whom everybody would recognize as owning his years and describe as "looking forty." Poncet was "well preserved."

" I have some letters for you," he said gaily,
before he could be greeted other than by
Mary's smile and gesture of invitation. " One
for madame," presenting it with a bow, "and
another for monsieur," and he held the business envelope out to Baylor's indifferent
fingers.

" Sit down, Poncet. Sit down and have a
cigar.   What's new in New York ? "

Baylor brought out a box of cigars, and saw
his visitor established before he turned to his
own letter.

Neither of them noticed Mary. She had
opened the envelope, after having first looked
at the address as though a recognition of the
handwriting were the only possible means she
could have of learning the writer, and then
had unfolded the sheet with curiosity. As she
saw the first words she drew in her breath with
a little gasp, and looked at her husband with
what was almost fear in her face. If Baylor
had seen it, it would have astonished him beyond words. Secrets and fears were unknown
between these two. Mary put the letter in

its envelope and tucked it under her belt, and gathering together the remnants of her hat materials, started to leave the room.

As she passed Baylor he looked up at her.

"Who was your letter from, Polly? Old Griggs? How is the old fellow?"

"Very well," Mary said in a constrained voice, and left the room. Outside she took the letter out and read it quickly, and then, her face white and anxious, tore it into small bits, and opening the window, let them fly out into the street.

II.

THE little rooms at Atlantic City were in an airy building attached to a bath house. The morning sun streamed in at the windows, and the wind brought the spray of the ocean, which lapped and rolled and pounded away as though it were inviting the world to come and play with it.

Mary dressed her baby in the dainty little garments her own fingers had fashioned while Mr. Baylor drank his coffee, which he always took in bed, and read over the morning paper.

" By Jove," he exclaimed, " here's our next door neighbor, staying at the hotel just behind us."

" Who ? Not — surely not Poncet from 276."

" My innocent child ! Our neighbors in these days mean the inhabitants of the sylvan

shades of Ellenbro'. Listen to this, in the
Atlantic City arrivals: 'General and Mrs.
Courtney, Mr. Reginald Courtney, and Miss
Smith.'

"Disguised under the plebeian name of
Smith, my dear Mary, is the richest girl in
our part of the country. She is the catch.
She has a broad face like a Holstein cow, and
is about as intelligent. But she is pure white.
She hasn't any black spots," added Mr. Baylor, as though he feared that Miss Smith
might be mistaken for the animal mentioned
unless he explained. "The Courtneys want
to catch her for Reginald, who isn't a half
bad fellow, and who does, I believe, like Miss
Smith first rate. My dear, good sister Eliza
supplied me with the current gossip of the
county when I saw her last. Good gracious,
Mary, do you think you can ever break into
the harness of going about and minding your
neighbors' business? Not that they'll be
likely to offer you the opportunity very soon.
We are black sheep, my dear, and it will probably be some time before we are taken into

the confidences of our first families down in
Ellenbro'. They never were very fond of me."

"And I," Mary said, flushing, "am entirely
out of it. Not that I care. But I am not
going to believe that people will not be kind
to me. I am sure I want everybody to have
his own good time in his own good way. I am
not going to pretend I am trying to be like
them. I *wouldn't* be!"

"You are better than the best of the lot,
my dear, and the reason I love you is because
you are such an everlasting simpleton. I
hope, for my own sake, that the old tabbies
never lick you into shape. It might be better
for Dolly to have a conventional mamma, seeing that it is likely that she will never have a
conventional papa. She will need somebody
to marry her off——"

"I will not be made over. I am *me*," said
Mrs. Baylor with fine scorn. "And Dolly will
need no one to marry her off."

"Mary, my love, you are developing a very
ill bred habit of interrupting people in the
middle of their sentences."

Baylor had lighted a cigar, and was in the midst of an editorial in a New York paper, but he was keeping one side of his indolent consciousness toward his wife.

"My ways may all be ill bred, according to your family's standards, but any way they are honest. I say exactly what I mean."

"And tell all you know."

A quick, embarrassed little flush came up into Mrs. Baylor's face, and she turned to little Dolly's bonnet, tying the strings with her face almost inside.

"I declare," Mr. Baylor said, "if McDonald hasn't gone and written up all that stuff I told him the other day about famous gamblers. And here it is, illustrated in this sheet. I suppose he thought he had to be remunerated for his losses at poker that last night."

"I *hate* gambling," Mary said vindictively.

Mr. Baylor declined to answer, and argument was senseless. Little Dolly was curled and dressed and bonneted by this time. Her mother turned her around and looked at her admiringly, as though she were a big doll.

"Go and kiss your papa by by, baby, and tell him he is a lazy thing not to go to breakfast with us! I know you don't want to take us down to Ellenbro'—we're a bother—but I'm *going!*" And Mrs. Baylor shuts the door with emphasis, as though her morning coffee lay in that new home she was so anxious to see.

III.

IT is still before noon. Up in one of the pavilions there is a little group of four. The sort of people who are always described as a "family party," the sort of people who are invariably recognized everywhere as being from "out of town," to their own eternal mystification.

They bought their clothes at the best establishments in New York, and yet nobody seemed to take them for New Yorkers. Not that they were particularly anxious to be known as city people. The name of Courtney was too well known in that part of the middle South where they lived for them to envy any man his habitation.

General Courtney, general of militia for twenty five years, was a large gentleman with a quiet manner and a good deal of gray hair, on head and lip. Mrs. Courtney, who would appear on her tombstone as his " beloved and respected wife," held her head up with the air of a woman who has her way in about every position in which she is thrown, an air calculated to impress the weak and cause mirth in the strong, instead of inciting them to battle, as is evidently sometimes Mrs. Courtney's intention.

Reginald Courtney is a fair type of a big, healthy, not overly wise young man, who treats the world he does not know with courtesy. The creases in his trousers are in the right place, and his shoes are correct, but there is no sophistication in his face. He is treasurer of a company for mining coal in the West Virginia hills, and there are signs that his face has known the sun. It is not a particularly handsome face, but the body below it is straight and sturdy and tall, and the head above it looks anything but empty. Reg has never had an ache since he was born, and if clean living and healthy ways are factors, he never will. He is one with whom the world seems to have gone well.

By his side sits the girl who, from her baby-hood, has been destined to become his wife. A distant cousin, born into one of the oldest families in the middle South, she has the un-usual good fortune to have an estate which even the civil war did not affect, so great and solid and well invested was it. An orphan, she inherited her whole fortune from her father's father, a canny old man, who had more English than American blood, and who left his entire estate to his son's eldest child, to be held in trust until the heir had reached the age of twenty five.

Edyth had been given into Mrs. Courtney's hands when she was only five, and had been brought up in the conventions of her class.

People in Virginia did not call her plain, although an irreverent Northerner, accustomed to the dash of city heiresses, might have thought so. There is too satisfied an expression in Miss Smith's face, although she is unaffected and simple in her manner.

She affects some sensitive souls much as an unripe peach might. She has not gained the ripeness and sweetness which comes with experience and the contact with the light of the world's day. She is a trifle overdressed. She is only twenty years old, but there are diamond earrings in her ears, and her gown is silk instead of cotton or wool, this summer morning by the sea.

Reginald, like all fine men, knows nothing whatever about women's dress, but some way Edyth doesn't look just right. He thinks vaguely that after they are married he will get her to go about with him alone and be more unconventional. There are few marriages made in which one or the other of the contracting parties does not intend to make some future alterations in the beloved one.

General Courtney sits with his face toward the board walk, looking into the visage of each passerby with that expectation of finding an acquaintance which never leaves a man who has been brought up in a country place where his own personality is distinct, however much he may travel about this overgrown world.

He started suddenly as a well dressed figure in white flannels and a broad sailor hat lounged along, and then, with a glance at his wife, sat down again.   The passerby was absorbed in his cigarette, and seemed to see nobody through his half closed eyes.

"Who was it?" Mrs. Courtney asked. "Any Ellenbro' people?"

"Well, yes, you might say so," the general said, as though he were apologizing for owning the fact. "It was Richard Baylor. Since he has inherited Castle Hill, I suppose we might call him a neighbor."

A look of superior virtue came over Mrs. Courtney's face, if anything could be superior to her usual exalted expression.

"I wonder," she said in a casual tone, "if—er—he is alone?"

"He was just now."

"It is to be sincerely hoped that he will not bring his—er—family down to Castle Hill."

"Why not?"   Mr. Reginald Courtney dashed into the conversation with an air that

was a trifle more than mildly curious. His
tone sounded as if he might already anticipate
the answer he would receive and was prepared
to take up an independent position in regard
to it. But his mother felt herself on indisput-
able heights.

"I hope, my son, that knowing, as you
must, the character borne by Richard Baylor,
and the unhappy marriage he has made, you
will readily understand why it is not desirable
that he should come to Ellenbro' and place
himself and his friends in the midst of our
community of gently bred people."

"Most of whom are related to him."

"Which makes it all the more unfortunate."

"I can't see what is so terrible about Baylor. From all I hear about him he is a clever
fellow, who has been in the swim of affairs
and mingled with people who were of consequence sufficiently to make a very comfortable
income as a newspaper writer. Nobody seems
to have anything to say about him except
that he plays poker too much. As for his

wife, I don't believe Baylor would have married anybody who wasn't pretty and nice and
young. I don't see why a nice, young, pretty
woman at Castle Hill will not be an acquisition."

Mrs. Courtney's face had settled into its
hardest lines.

" I can hardly consider a young woman who
was picked up at the stage door, one might
say, as an acquisition to Ellenbro' and the
county. However sorry I shall feel for dear
Eliza, I still have my *principles*—my duty—
and I cannot see how these are to be overcome
sufficiently for me to recognize Richard Baylor's wife."

" Well, now, mother, you are flying right in
the face of all modern ideas. There was a
time when an actress was not a social light,
but that time has gone by long ago. They
are asked everywhere, especially in London,
which you say is the only properly regulated
city on earth. They make a point of having
actors at the very best houses. The Prince
of Wales——"

"I hope," said Mrs. Courtney, in a tone which would have done credit to the British matron herself, "that *my* son will never look upon the moral character of the Prince of Wales as a model. I am very sure that his dear mother has never entertained actresses." Mrs. Courtney spoke the word as though it was a medical term, necessary to use, but rather indelicate.

"Is there anything wrong with Mrs. Baylor's moral character?"

Edyth was looking out over the ocean as though she had heard none of the conversation, but Mrs. Courtney looked at her and back to her son warningly, but the irrepressible went on.

"Because if there isn't, I think we might be glad to know her. We are pretty well acquainted with Mrs. Chapin."

"Reginald, if you have any unpleasant allusions to make, I must request you to confine them to the hours when you are not in Edyth's society, *at least*. I suppose you men may act as you please. If you find

Richard Baylor agreeable, nothing *we* may say will prevent your seeking his society. I hope you have too much strength of mind to be drawn into his wretched habit of gambling, and I trust you will remain away from his house."

"And Mrs. Baylor is to get all the cold shoulder. I don't call that justice exactly. She wasn't on the stage, any way. She only studied for the stage. Plenty society women have gone through that school."

"I think you can hardly call it the same thing. As I understand it, this Mrs. Baylor is the daughter of an actress, and had a sister who was on the stage for a time, in a very inferior position, until she made a miserable marriage and died in Paris."

"Oh, Aunt Martha," Miss Smith called, in a low but excited tone, "here is that lady we saw yesterday. It must be Mrs. Colonel Stanley; she answers exactly to the description I read of her in the papers yesterday. Look at her go into the water. Did you ever see anything so graceful?"

Mrs. Courtney put up her lorgnette and

watched the slim, perfectly clad figure walk like a princess down over the sands and into the water. Her bathing dress fitted her figure like the tunic of a young Greek, and the proud neck upheld the beautifully carried head with a conspicuous pride. There was no timid stopping to dillydally with the waves, to put one foot out and then another, and draw back with a little shiver. She walked almost up to the water, and then with a rush went straight into the heart of a great, white crested breaker, coming up with her face wet, but brilliant.

She gave two or three strokes with her round, strong, white arms, and made her way out into the incoming swells, and then, as a great, green, glassy wave rose above her, ready to sweep over her head, she put her hands on her waist, and springing with the motion of the water, rose above it, bounding into the air. Her scarlet cap rose two or three times, defying the waves to go over it, and then it went out, a touch of color as far as it could be seen.

" I should think she would be afraid," Edyth said, almost shivering.

"The Lacys are a fearless race," Mrs. Courtney replied, as one would repeat history. " I can remember that old General Lacy was said to be the bravest man in the army. He was a second cousin of your grandfather Mason, Reginald. It is the same blood. There have never been any cowards in our families. It that really is Helen Stanley, we certainly must go and call upon her. It would be very strange if relatives should be in the same city and not see each other."

" From what I hear of Mrs. Colonel Stanley, and from what the newspapers say of her, I reckon she has about enough occupation in attending to the many friends she has now. They say she came down here, where she knows nobody, so that she might have the sea bathing and not be annoyed by people."

"We can hardly be considered in the light of people. Her own kin!"

Mrs. Courtney was rapidly losing her temper with her son.

"She is a remarkable swimmer," said General Courtney, putting up the field glass, which he considered an indispensable addition to a seaside toilet. It is supposed that he imbibed the idea from reading of old sea captains and their glasses. Most worldly experiences had come to General Courtney vicariously.

"But, dear me, Helen Lacy, old Bob Lacy's daughter, must be forty, if she's a day. Her mother——"

"Not so old as that," begins Mrs. Courtney, when her son Reginald gives her another turn.

"We aren't at all sure that it is Mrs. Stanley at all. People seldom look like their reputations. This may be one of those very actresses you so despise."

"I trust I know a lady when I see one," says his mother with dignity. "It is not very complimentary to say that your cousin, Mrs. Stanley, looks like an actress."

"She's not so near a cousin that I feel as though I were exactly casting aspersions upon my immediate family."

" And then, too, you seem to have taken up the cudgels in defense of that scapegrace, Richard Baylor."

It is a minute before Reginald speaks, and then there is feeling in his voice.

" It seems to me, mother, that we need to add to, instead of detract from, the stock of sympathy in this world for scapegraces."

And he leaves his mother dumb.

" Come along, Edyth, let us go off and walk a little. My knees are getting cramped by sitting still," and Reginald gets up and gives his tan shoes a little shake that straightens his trousers, and presumably his knees.

Edyth follows him obediently. Where wouldn't she follow Reginald? Her heart is as full of joy as the sea, laughing and glittering away off there to the eastern horizon, is full of sparkles. It is reflecting back the light which the indifferent sun is pouring down on all the earth alike, and the sea's case is something like poor Edyth's. Reginald is in as little lover-like a mood as possible.

He knows that he is going to ask Edyth to

marry him. Of course he is. He knows that his mother expects it, and, most of all, Edyth expects it. He thinks, with a quick throb of conscience, of the stab he has given his mother before he left. He hates himself for his defiant tongue. He knows that he cannot go and apologize to her, because the apology would be but a naming of the wound, and demanding for it a new claim upon the consciousness, and it is something that must be kept hidden away.

With his impulsive generosity, he makes up his mind that now, today, he will make amends to his mother, carry out her dearest wishes, and go back to her with Edyth as his promised wife. She will forgive him then for his rude touch upon the family sorrow, the skeleton which can hurt even Mrs. Courtney's pride. Her kiss of congratulation will be a kiss of reconciliation. He thinks ruefully that it is his duty to make up to his mother all she has suffered.

But what can he say to Edyth? He thinks to himself that certainly nothing on earth could be harder than to propose marriage to a girl who has been brought up in the same house with you. It is perfectly ridiculous.

When Edyth, a shy little child of five, was left to General Courtney's guardianship, Mrs. Courtney announced to the world that she took up the burden of being a mother to a motherless girl in a spirit of Christian charity. She openly wished that this child had been a boy, that Reg might have had a companion, and then she said she supposed it was all for the best, as poor Reg had no sister; the refining influence of a girl in the house would be everything.

And true enough, Mrs. Courtney did her duty in the way of the world. Edyth had been daintily and carefully brought up, with the best of young ladies' boarding school educations. She had been taught art embroidery as the years went by, and the making of famous Virginia dishes, and the painting of china to put them in.

But it must be confessed that poor Edyth had never done any of these things very brilliantly. She could hardly be said to have any influence over Reg, although they were together constantly during all their childhood. Reginald had never had but one girl companion other than Edyth, and that was a pretty miss of ten who had come out from Baltimore to visit her aunt who lived near the Courtneys. Reginald was fourteen and Edyth was eleven when Maude appeared on the scene and took Reg's boyish heart captive. She could ride and swim and row and climb trees like a boy, and had a sharp tongue of her own; in none of which accomplishments Edyth was at all learned.

Reg was her willing slave until they were riding tournament on the back lawn one day. Maude, on her pony bareback and yelling like a Comanche Indian, galloping down with lance poised to take the ring, found herself almost thrown because her pony had shied at Edyth's white apron, when she sat on the fence meekly looking on. Maude had called her a "spoil sport" and ordered her home. Reg picked up the rings and went along, much to Mrs. Courtney's satisfaction when she heard of it.

She would hardly have been a human mother if she had not wanted to keep Edyth's thirty thousand dollars a year in the family; if she had not gently discouraged any other man who came Edyth's way. Not that that required much effort. The American man is not a fortune hunter. He has too much faith in his own abilities, is too proud to take a wife's money. He considers it his prerogative as an American to earn his own fortune and to choose the one woman he wants out of the world to bestow it upon.

Edyth, with her rather awkward figure and stiffness of manner, had little to attract any man, particularly one who did not really know her good qualities. She always had partners at dances and never had known the ignominy of being a wall flower. Everybody went to the Courtney house, and liked Reginald, and one dance is little to give for duty; but Edyth, with the handsomest gown in the room, had never been a belle.

To do Reginald justice, he never thought
of Edyth's money. It is hard to think of
money in connection with one for whom it
has done so little. He only knew that she
was good, that she was devoted to him, that
his mother would be heartbroken if he married any one else, and that he had never seen
any other woman whom he cared any more
for.

Not that bright eyes and a pretty face had
no charms for him. He was a young man
with blood in his veins, and eyes in his head,
and when a gay, bright young girl, full of the
joy of life, passed him by, his heart gave an
extra throb in the manner that every healthy
young man's does at that call. But the only
girls he had ever known were those about his
own home, and in their eyes, as in his
mother's, he was the property of Edyth
Smith.

Tell a man a thing is a fact from his boyhood up, and he is certain to end by believ-
ing it.

Reg thought he loved Edyth. He had

never known a man who was passionately in love with his wife. The uncles and cousins, more or less removed, who made up the world about Ellenbro' all had wives very much like Edyth, good and commonplace. It was hardly in good taste to be anything else. And upon this frame of mind was destined to be embroidered the acquaintance of Mary Baylor.

Reg and Edyth walked along up the board walk side by side. The merry go rounds were grinding out their new tunes put in for this season, but only a stray boy and girl were seated upon the splendid and ferocious wooden tigers and lions, going round and round. Away out at sea the red cap of the swimmer they had seen go in, rose and fell on the waves. There was a memory of her poetry of motion in Reginald's mind.

"Forty!" he said to himself contemptuously. "Mrs. Stanley or no Mrs. Stanley, if *that* woman is forty, I'm seventy five."

Edyth broke into his reveries.

" Here's the iron pier. Let us walk out and look at the ocean."

"All right," is Reginald's invariable answer, and they turn to the right and walk out on the high pier. There is a small theater at the other end, but there is nobody there at this hour of the day. The rows of chairs sit empty like a wooden audience, waiting for performers that do not come.

There are some young girls who are made prettier by the fresh air of the ocean and the sunshine. The wind ruffles their hair in crisp little curls around foreheads and necks and ears, and gives their hats a saucy tilt that is the acme of coquetry. It brings deeper color into rounded cheeks, and prints a dear little brown freckle here and there on a white skin.

But Edyth is not one of these. The wind makes her look untidy, and that is all. The extra color that comes is in her nose and chin. Her lips look blue and her eyes are watery instead of laughing back to the sun. Reginald considerately suggests that they should get behind the theater where the wind is not so strong, and Edyth sits down on one of the red wooden seats.

Away off on the board walk a popular ditty plays an accompaniment. Now, thinks Reginald, he will say the necessary words.

He looks out at the little boats which are bluefishing outside the bar, the sun making their dingy sails white; he gives ear to the music; he turns his eyes to Edyth's face, and some way his courage dies.

"How big the world is, and yet how little," says Miss Smith. "To think of Uncle Mason seeing Mr. Baylor here. I hope we can get a subscription for the hospital from him. Shouldn't you think so?"

Reg isn't exactly interested in hospitals; like most young men, he thinks of the pleasant things of life, but he has a tenderness for Edyth's kind heart. The hospital is her pet charity, and the mention of it makes him think how womanly she is, and what a good wife she will make.

"I hope you don't want to go rushing after him now to get his name down on your little book."

"No, not now," she says. "I want to go

on to New York with Aunt Martha and get some new gowns before we go back home, and some new curtains for my own room."

"You love the old house at home very much, don't you, Edyth?" There is nothing remarkable about this question, but there is something strained in the tone in which it is put.

She looks at him, and knows that the time has come, and the slow red, not the vivid rushing blush that is so beautiful, comes into her face.

This moment is the most blissful of her dull life—this moment that it seems to Reg is about the most difficult he has ever encountered.

"Yes," she almost whispers.

"Wouldn't you—wouldn't you like to live there *always?*"

It is like pulling a tooth.

"You know I should be unhappy away from you—all."

And then, there seemed to be nothing more to be said. He puts his arm around her shoul-

ders and kisses her—and is conscious as he
does so that a hair has blown across her
lips, and he doesn't like it. He doesn't
even know, poor boy, that if that hair had
been blown across the lips of a woman he truly
loved, and had crossed his when he kissed her
first, it would have had a locket home for the
rest of its days.

There seems to be nothing else to say. They
both look out over the sea.

" I wonder what Aunt Martha will say when
we go in?"

"Must I tell her now—right off?" asks
Reg. Now that it is done, somehow it seems
as though it would keep.

" Of course it is *yours* to tell," she says with
an attempt at playfulness that is unlike her
and not desirable.

" I'll tell you what let's do," Reg said with
an air of inspiration. "Let's go into that
bath house and get some suits and go in
bathing."

Why not begin right now to start Edyth in
his ways?

IV.

IT must be confessed that the bathing suit which covers the slender figure of Miss Edyth Smith leaves considerable to be desired. It isn't pretty and it isn't trig.

She opens the door a little way and peeps out, and then looks longingly at her gown hanging up there. A boy suddenly bangs at her door.

"What do you want?" she asks timidly.

"The gen'leman said you was to come along. He's waitin'."

And then Edyth brought out all of her courage, opened the door and stepped out.

As they came down on the beach they saw that everybody was looking at a child who was frolicking in the water. She was a tiny little yellow headed baby, not more than three, but who could swim like a fish. There was a heavy faced woman with her who was evidently her nurse, and who was bursting with gratified vanity at the attention the baby was attracting. The child had a scrap of a bathing suit about its round little body, but she sprang into the incoming waves shouting with glee, putting her tiny hands upon her waist and rising above the breakers as it sprang into the flying spray.

"She springs up like Mrs. Stanley; look at her," Edyth cried, forgetting all about herself.

The child threw herself upon the next wave that came in, and put out her tiny arms and went swimming like a white, golden haired frog.

"I think that is dangerous," Reg said. "I do not believe that nurse can swim a stroke, and that baby has not the strength to cope with waves," and taking Edyth by the hand he started into the water. But the water was cold to Miss Smith's feet, and she stopped.

"Oh, Reginald, I *can't!* *Oh!*"

"Yes, you can. Look at all these people. It isn't cold after you get in. Come along."

"Oh! *Ugh!* I can*not!*"

People about them were beginning to laugh.

Reg was a sturdy soul, without a grain of
snobbery, but as he looked at Edyth he did
wish she were prettier, if she were going to be
silly, or more sensible and braver if she had to
be ugly. He put his arms about her waist
and rushed her into the incoming breaker,
lifting her head and shoulders above it.

"Oh—ah!" she gasped, and burst into tears.

Then I am afraid Reg felt his patience
going. "If you really cannot stand it——" he
said in the superhumanly mild tone of a man
in a real rage—but the waves do not wait for
arguments; another one came, and they let
themselves be washed nearly back upon the
beach.

There was a shriek almost in Reg's ear:
"The baby! Oh, the baby!"

It was the Irish nurse. She was wringing
her hands. "*Save her!*" she cried.

There were not many bathers in here, only
one or two men.

Reg turned to see the little golden head
away out on the top of a wave. Coming towards the shore still a distance out, was the

red cap of the swimmer they had seen go in
far up the beach. It was coming in rapidly,
but that baby could never live in those waves
until the red cap could reach her. Reg fairly
rushed into the water, leaving Edyth dripping
on the shore. It was not hard work for his
strong arms, but it seemed to him that he
would never reach the child nor find her when
he got there. The fatal undertow would make
short work of that soft atom.

A great green wall came up before him, and
in it, under it, he saw the white baby face, the
little arms helpless. He dived, grasped the
golden curls, and came up, holding himself
aloft on the sweep of the incoming tide, the
baby in his arms.

In another second the red cap was beside
him. Such an agonized face, the big eyes
wide. "My baby," she gasped.

"She's all right," Reg said, and truly enough
she was. The little thing had held her breath
under the water and breathed on top, with the
true instinct of a born swimmer, who had been
trained to the water before she could walk.

"I come to your cap, mamma," she said, shaking the water from her head like a dog.

It was no time for talk. The gratitude in the mother's eyes was more eloquent than any words.

Reg put the child astride his neck, and together he and the mother slowly swam in shore. The Irish nurse was gone. When they reached the sand and put the child down, the mother turned to Reg with tears in her pretty eyes.

"You saved my baby's life," she said.

There was a look in those eyes under the red cap which was dangerous for Reg. There are some women born with a *something* (other women call it coquetry sometimes, and sometimes they call it brazenness) which is fatal to nine men out of every ten who look at them.

No wonder was it that Mrs. Stanley was the great society leader. The few people who had been along the beach were all looking at them curiously. Edyth had only seen and felt that Reg had left her, and had turned and gone up the beach and into the bath house to don again the garments of her everyday walks, to bedeck herself with trinkets and be the Edyth of conventionality—except—except—in this one respect. There was upon her a new dignity. She was engaged to Reg. It looked all sunny before her now — and although she was cold, and the coarse flannel of the bathing suit was unpleasant to her skin, and the one towel was insufficient, still none of these could entirely hide the sun for Edyth, on this the day when the fruition of all her maidenly dreams had come about.

She even laughed at herself for a silly goose for having cried in the water. She would go in again tomorrow. Of course Reg was big enough and bold enough to take care of her, and she ought not to be so stupid. She wondered if Reg really meant that they were to keep their engagement for a month, and not tell even Mrs. Courtney. She didn't see how she could, and then she thrilled all over at the thought of having a great secret like that, that meant so much to them both, all alone with Reg.

She started out to find Reg. She thought
of sending a boy, but she suddenly bethought
herself that Mr. Reginald Courtney might not
be so conspicuous a personage along the sands
of Atlantic City as he would be in the streets
of Ellenbro'. The sense of lost identity is
one of the hardest lessons that provincials
must learn. She set her hat, her most expen-
sive hat, on her head, and taking her umbrella,
went out and sat in the pavilion which overlooked the bathers. Just as she appeared a
red cap, closely followed by a tall young man,
crossed the sands, went up the stairs, and
separating with a tacit promise in each face to
meet again in a very few minutes, the two
went into their several dressing rooms.

There was nothing of the gallant about
Reginald Courtney, but when that merry
piquant face under the red cap was turned to
him, he forgot that she was a stranger.

"Must you go out?" he said. It wasn't
every day that a swimmer like this could keep
stroke beside him.

"The nurse has gone, and I must go and

dress the baby. She has been in too long now. Poor little tot! I never intended for her to come into the water at all this morning. I have never had a nurse for her in all her little life before, but her papa thinks she ought to have one so that we may have more time for other things. Just as though anything could be more important than having the baby with us!"

"Me won't go out!" said a small but defiant voice.

"Sh—h. Don't speak to your mamma like that!" There was anything but severity in the soft tones, but the baby changed her cry.

"I see my papa!" she shrieked, and breaking away from her mother, tore through the crowd, a little bundle of pink flesh, wet flannel, and stringy curls.

Reg did not wait to hear the thanks of the head of the family; it seemed to him that that was a formality that he could deny himself. With a hasty word of farewell, he started up towards the place where he had left Edyth. She was gone. He went up to the bath house, and found that she had taken the key of her dressing room. Reg knew from many years' experience that when Edyth began to dress, it was a matter of labor and painstaking, and *time*. He looked longingly back at the glittering, heaving waves, rushing in so coolly and enticingly. Did his eyes deceive him? Away out there on the crest of one of them was a red cap. That decided him. In another minute his strong white arms and close cropped head were making their way through the breakers towards that scarlet beacon.

"I'll tell her this time," Reg thinks to himself, "that we are cousins. I'll talk to her, and it naturally will come into the conversation."

She was out there all alone, as he had hoped, and the face she turned towards him was as cordial and gay as it had been when he left it. Some way it made Reg into a hero. It made his swim to the rescue of that small girl, and his grasp upon her curls, seem the act of a great man. The glance in those eyes, sweet

as it was, seemed to act like a magnifier. It
made Reg swell in importance.

"Where did you go to?" she cried, as she
threw herself upon the wave, passively, as
another woman would throw herself upon a
silken couch for a languid summer afternoon's
rest. Her round white arms, slender, yet with
dimples in the elbows, and a dear little crease
on the forearm just below the bend that enticed you to kiss it, were spread out, and the
water seemed to hold her up and support her
upon its heaving green bosom as though it
loved her.

"I went up to see what had become of my—
my cousin. But she was dressing."

She laughed. "And you knew that meant
another hour! I am so glad you came back. I
wanted you to stay and meet my husband.
He might have said some *words* that could
have given you some idea of our thanks. I
could not."

"You thanked me enough," Reg said. "It
was nothing."

"Nothing, to save my baby's life? It probably seemed nothing to you. You may go about saving lives every day in the week, for aught I know—but my *baby!*"

The words sounded a little flippant, but there was a ghost of a sob at the end, and the water on the round delicate cheeks was not all ocean's brine. It thrilled Reg to the heart. He never stopped to think how cross he had been to Edyth for crying just a little while ago.

"Did the nurse come back?" he asked—for something to say.

"Yes; her father said he would stay with her while the nurse dressed her. She seemed awfully repentant, poor thing, and I could hardly blame her." She laughed again, that merry laugh that seemed to come out for its own enjoyment, showing all the white teeth and the depressed corners of the not very small nor thin lipped mouth. "It is more than I can do to resist that child's pleading. How can I expect a nurse to do it?"

"I don't wonder," Reg said, and then he blushed. It seemed to him that anybody would give this woman anything she wanted, why not her child?

But the red cap had other occupation than listening to the flatteries of a boy. She had come out to bathe, to swim and dive, and feel the cool waves break over her, and she went vigorously to work, untiring, seemingly.

When at last they came out, just as Edyth, her hair a little wet, and not so daintily arranged as before, took her chair in the pavilion and turned it oceanward, they felt that they had been friends forever. There was an Irishwoman, meek of mien, holding fast to a dancing, golden haired little girl, very near them.

"Your mamma has come out now, I'm tellin' ye," said the nurse. "Didn't ye see her red cap a-comin' up out o' the water? She's jest in the house beyant a dressin' an' will be here the minute—an' it's glad I am," under her breath.

Edyth pricked up her ears at the mention of the red cap. She had seen only one, and that was on Mrs. Stanley's head. Could this

be Mrs. Stanley's little girl? She turned and
smiled upon the infant. That was enough;
in two minutes her bangle bracelets were
being closely inspected.

Edyth's array of bangles was large. There
was a little gold pig, a *porte bonheur*, which
set the child screaming with delight. "The
pid! the pid! The pitty pid!"

Just then a lady, in a simple, cool white
gown came in at the pavilion gate. Reg was
just behind her, looking red and fresh. The
baby sprang for her. "Mamma," she cried,
"come and see the lady with the pid." Edyth
recognized her; it was Mrs. Stanley.

"I hope you will pardon my little girl," she
said very sweetly. "She wants everything
she sees. I am afraid she is frightfully
spoiled."

"Oh, no!" Edyth said. "Let me give it
to her. I should be glad for her to have it,"
and she began unhooking it from her bracelet.
There is a hand put out to stop her.

"I cannot allow her——" but the air is
rent by a shrill wail.

" I wants th' *pid !* "

" Please let her have it," Edyth says almost imploringly. " It isn't like taking it from a *stranger.* I fancy we are almost cousins," hurrying on, as she sees the wonder in the face before her. Reg has come up, and Edyth turns toward him to second her. " We are the Courtneys from Ellenbro'." She always speaks of herself as a Courtney.

" Ah ! " and a pleased flush came into the face under the red cap. " Do you know me then ? "

Coming toward them Edyth sees Mrs. Courtney, and knows from her face that she, too, sees Mrs. Stanley.

" Why, of course, Aunt Martha knew you at once, and said we must come and see you."

" I will tell Dick." There is a little triumph in the tone. " You might have recognized *him*, but I cannot understand how you could know that I am *Mrs.* Richard Baylor ! "

V.

A YOUNG girl brought up in the country often acquires a self possession that a city girl of the same age totally lacks. There is a coming and going among the old families who have many branches which gives a daughter of a large connection an ease and tact in dealing with people of all sorts, a readiness, which the city girl, who has depended on her mother for everything, rarely has until she is fairly launched into the world upon her own account, when the very goddesses would stand abashed at her uplifted head and grand carriage. All the experience had come to Edyth, but her nature had been unfruitful ground. She had profited by none of it. As she looks at Mary and realizes the awful mistake she has made, she would gladly seek the watery depths of one of the great waves, and come up oblivious to her surroundings.

Mary reads with unerring instinct the change in Edyth's expression, and after the first sharp little scratch of mortification she rather enjoys the situation.

"Oh, yes!" Edyth falters, " I—we—Aunt Martha knows Miss Eliza Baylor very well. I think—Reg, I am sure aunt is looking for us—I see her coming," and Edyth half turns. But Reg has brought a chair out with something of a bang, and has plainly made up his mind to seat himself and stay where he is. Edyth may defy some things, but, unassisted, she cannot defy that expression in the face of the man who is her lord and master.

In spite of herself she sits down. Mary spreads her crisp white skirt and looks her blandly and smilingly in the face. Nearer and nearer comes Mrs. Courtney, and while Mary's smile may be bland, Mrs. Courtney's is positively buttery. Her feeling at seeing Edyth and Reginald there by the side of Mrs. Stanley is one of genuine gratification.

Mrs. Stanley is a woman who is always mentioned with pride by the Southern people,

who jealously guard the traditions of their
section. She has married a rich man of social
standing, and being gay and good natured and
popular, has made much of her position, and
is one of the women whose name and photograph (or rather the caricature which is called
a newspaper photograph)are constantly appear-
ing in print. She has had years of attention,
and the novelty having worn off to some extent, she seeks few of her compatriots. While
the world of the Northern cities—her social
world—has year by year taken on new ways
of amusing itself, has been growing lighter
and lighter in tone, has ceased to contemplate
itself too closely, and has gone far afield for
some of its diversions, the class from which
she came in the South still holds many of the
traditions of an earlier time. They may be
amusing enough to look at from a distance, but
to live with them even for a day tries Mrs.
Stanley's patience.

Mrs. Courtney understands none of this.
Her comprehension is limited to the fact that
few people she knows ever see anything of

Mrs. Stanley. The opportunity has come to her. She almost hears herself telling her old friends at home all about it.

Edyth is dyed crimson with mortification, and feels a dreadful temptation to hold her tongue, even as Mrs. Courtney's expansive person turns in through the narrow door of the pavilion and comes sweeping toward them. She feels her own utter incapacity to shape events, and the cowardice which takes refuge in silence possesses her.

Mrs. Courtney's smile is so effusive, so motherly, that Edyth arises and tries to give her some sort of a hint. She says:

"Oh, here is Aunt Martha! She has come for us," and she starts toward Mrs. Courtney to arrest her in midair as it were. But Mrs. Courtney is too heavy a projectile for any such frivolous turning aside.

"Such a pleasure to meet you here," she says, advancing upon Mary with outstretched hand. "It is so seldom any of us find any of our own people in the North. I am delighted that the children discovered you."

"I am covered with gratitude that they found me, too," Mary says. "I feel like thanking you for having a son. If it had not been for him I am afraid I should not have had a daughter today," and she hugged the little girl up in her strong arms.

Mrs. Courtney looked questioningly at Reg, and he looked out at sea as though he were not at all interested in the conversation.

"He saved my baby's life."

"I am sure he did a good deed for the world. Such a beautiful child!" Mrs. Courtney sits down and puts out her tightly gloved hand coaxingly towards the spoiled Dolly.

"Go 'way!" says that piece of tactless impertinence.

"How much she looks like her grandmother Lacy! Such a beautiful woman that she was! You must get the general to tell you of the famous old tales they tell of her. How she was the toast of the county. Your little girl bids fair to be just such another great beauty."

There is first a puzzled look, and then artless Mary begins to believe that Mrs. Courtney means to be kind. She is the mother of this splendid young man; he must have taken his nature from her.

"I never heard," she says, "of Dolly's grandmother Lacy. Richard has not told me much of the family. I am glad Dolly is going to have an inheritance of beauty. I have always thought it must be behind her *somewhere*." Mary laughs as if in deprecation of her own charms.

"Not know——" Mrs. Courtney wonders if Helen Stanley has even forgotten her own mother.

Edyth rushes in. "It is all my fault, Aunt Martha. You did not understand. This is—is—Mrs. Richard Baylor."

The dull red of extreme embarrassment takes the field of Mrs. Courtney's cheeks.

"I cannot see where your fault comes in, Edyth," Reginald says. "It seems to me a very fortunate thing for all of us to have made the acquaintance of Mrs. Baylor here and now.

I am sure I am everlastingly grateful to little Dolly for getting out of her depth."

Mrs. Courtney rises, and as she lifts her hand, it acts as a signal for Edyth, who follows her.

"I really must beg your pardon, madam, for my most unfortunate mistake. Through some inadvertence the children seem to have mistaken you for a relative of our own." Mrs. Courtney looks at Mary slightingly, as though *she* could never have made any such mistake. "Come, my dear." She puts her hand in Edyth's arm and draws her gently away.

Poor Mary! Slights have not come much in her way in the course of her young life, spent among her own sort. The little flat has been her kingdom since she was married, and before that, why, the wide world—her world seemed to be hers. With the instinct of any hurt creature seeking help, she turns and looks at Reginald. Men never had deserted her. Would this one? Her look was potent.

It was this that had cut Mary Baylor out for the stage all those years ago; it was this that

had made old Marshall, the manager, vow she
should have a theater and a play of her very
own to play in.   It was this that night when
they were having a dress rehearsal—how long
ago it all seemed—which went straight through
the blasé veneer which enwrapped Richard
Baylor, cynical, man of the world Dick Baylor,
and pierced his heart.   It was this not to be
understood *something* which had kept him
dangling at the heels of a chit of a girl who
hadn't even made her début; that kept him
buying flowers and candy where he had once
bought champagne.   It was this that called
him back after he had been driven away from
the young actress, by her sharp refusal of any
more of his attentions.   It was this that had
made him do a thing he had never expected
to do in all his life—ask this young girl to
marry him.

Dozens had gone down under it since, coming up to it conscious of its power.   To poor
country bred Reg a look like this was like fire
to the traditional tow.   His heart went like a
trip hammer.   Edyth, his recent vows, mother,

everything were forgotten in the rush that went over him with that look.

Reginald is alone with Mrs. Baylor. He is as heartily ashamed of his family as it is possible for a man to be. With all the American hatred of snobbery in any form, with all the enthusiasm of youth aroused in behalf of a woman who seems to be a special point of attack for her own sex, Reg is a champion whom any woman might be glad to have enter the lists for her. It is a tactless and shortsighted mother and sweetheart who have forced him into taking this position.

He cannot apologize for them. He can only show his own feeling ; and Reg is not the man to do anything by halves. Now he seats himself by Mrs. Baylor with the air of an old friend. He isn't sure that he does not feel easier with her when he knows that she is Mrs. Baylor than he did while he thought her Mrs. Stanley. It is a sad fact that when a natural man—a man who isn't a prig—finds himself in Bohemian environment, he feels happy.

They ignore the incident that has just passed. There is no trace of it, except perhaps in an added warmth in the manner of both. Mary wishes to show Reg her gratitude, and Reg wishes to bring out his own independence and the admiration he really feels for the little woman. He sits and talks to her for an hour, and then when she starts home he goes with her. Mrs. Courtney and Edyth are sitting out on their hotel veranda. Mrs. Courtney slowly waves a big black feather fan in the ocean breeze. It is so cool that it is hardly necessary, but the long plumes seem to give a funereal dignity to her whole expression. Her gown is heavily jetted, and the squeak of the tight silk and the rattle of the bugles make one think of trappings and harness.

Edyth has had time to make some changes in her own dress. There were so few really good opportunities for dressing in Ellenbro' that they missed no chance to put on fresh adorning here. As Edyth stood before her mirror she had dabbed away a suspicion of a tear, and covered up the telltale red mark with a rub of powder. She had a lonely feeling, although her engagement was not two hours old. As she sits there on the veranda, she sees Reg, surely her own Reg, coming sauntering, not walking along as though he had been pressed into service and was only doing a duty toward an acquaintance, but leaning down, interested, forgetting everything except the sight of his companion's face—and that companion was Mrs. Baylor.

Mrs. Courtney waved her fan more majestically than ever.

"My dear Edyth," she said, "I *hope* you see *now* why I so abruptly declined any acquaintance with Mrs. Baylor whatsoever. There is given to some women an evil influence which this one appears to possess. I thank heaven that *I* was never such a one!"

Young Mr. Courtney was being admirably entertained. Mary had never seen any reason on earth why she should not make herself as agreeable as possible to every one with whom she came in contact. She was like the mirror which gives back smiles for smiles, and her smile was always ready.

When it was there exactly before Reg, with all its beauty and bloom and attraction for him, he was quite oblivious to the fact that his mother and sweetheart were watching all his ways from the hotel veranda. Indeed, he never knew when he passed them.

Mary is telling him all sorts of incidents, called up by people who have passed them—when suddenly she makes a little dive and touches on the arm a very foreign looking man with black eyes. He is dressed very correctly, and his hair—thin to be sure—is accurately parted in the center, and brushed down before his ears, in the true fashion of the boulevardier of the last decade. He isn't young in years—but no decay has begun to show in his spirit.

"Such luck!" cried Mary, with what seems to Reg a disproportionate amount of gladness in her voice. "I knew you couldn't stay away from us for any length of time."

"Where is my young sweetheart, my lady love?"

"Dolly? Oh, she is——" Mary turns. "I though she was following us with her nurse, but it seems she isn't. I suppose she has picked up her papa somewhere. Where did you—— I beg your pardon, Mr. Courtney; I must introduce you to almost my very oldest friend, Mr. Poncet, our next door neighbor in New York. My dear little home in New York! I hope you are treating it well?"

"But it is disconsolate without you."

An expression of real sadness came over Mary's face.

"Do you know, Mr. Courtney," she said, "that when it came to tearing up my little apartment in New York I simply could not do it. It was our little *home*. I felt that it must stay there for us to go back to. Of course it was a piece of great extravagance to go on paying the rent when we were not going to live there, but my husband humored me. I suppose I shall get over it presently when Ellenbro' gets to be my home, and I can stand it to have the things brought down a few at a time—and then some day I suppose the little nest we made there will be like the bedroom I had when I was a girl : something to remember, but not regret."

"Madame is very prettily sentimental," old Poncet said with his best air.

"Where are you staying?" Mary asks.

"At the Mangate, the large hotel. It is the only one. The only one where you can get a respectable dinner at six or seven o'clock in the evening. At the others they expect you to dine at two," and there is scorn on the countenance of Mr. Poncet. "Where are you?"

"Oh, we are at some rooms about here that one of our friends told us of last year. We go out for our dinner. Sometimes here— sometimes there—like the pair of Bohemians we are, but Dick said this morning he believed he would go to a hotel. We have no parlor, and now that we have some friends here "— her smile included them both—" we shall want a spot where we can entertain them. The Windermere, for instance. Where are you, Mr. Courtney?"

"We are staying there."

" Are you ? Isn't that jolly ! "

" They are going to have a dance there to-night," Mr. Poncet says casually. " And I shall of course expect the honor."

"Which you shall certainly have. Oh, I think we shall come over there ourselves. I'll ask Dick about it as soon as he comes in. Here I am at home." She holds out her two pretty hands, one to each of the men. They are ungloved, and the action is by no means conventional, but nobody thinks of that. Then she gaily nods, and gives a backward look to Reg. " I'll expect to have a dance with you tonight, too, Mr. Courtney," and Reg lifts his hat and answers that he will think of nothing else all day. He is nearer telling the truth than most people are who make a gallant remark.

He leaves Mr. Poncet, he hardly knows how. He has a vague idea afterwards that the other must have seen the nurse coming with Dolly and gone up to meet them. Any way, he finds himself strolling back towards the hotel with his consciousness full of Mrs.

Baylor and that light sense of well being which comes to us when we have the anticipation of happy hours.

Suddenly there is a little chill in his happiness. He wonders if Edyth is thinking of going to that dance. Edyth rather enjoys dancing, and Reg has a remembrance that when they go together she is seldom taken off his hands for long at a time. Edyth isn't one of the girls who charms a man into forgetting that time flies and probably other men want to dance with her. A little of the stubborn look which his mother knows so well comes into Reg's face. Why is he engaged to Edyth any way? *Is* he? Then every bit of manliness there is in the boy comes out, and he remembers tenderly Edyth's love for him, and how good and true a girl she is, and he tells himself that he is an ungrateful brute and that he loves her and is proud and glad that they are going to be married ; but—he does hope that she will not want to go to the dance.

After all Reginald is *himself.* Why, because a man is engaged, must he be tied to one

woman's apron string?   It is all because they
had lived down in that little country town and
have known nothing of the world and its ways,
that a man is socially dead and buried when
he is married.   He remembers Madame Bona-
parte's scornful description of Baltimore
society, that "men only went into it to seek
a wife."

Reg goes home and into his own room,
where he throws off his coat and lies down to a
cigar and a novel.   He is an active young
fellow, but he seems to have enough to think
about to supply him with exercise.   His
mother comes and knocks at his locked door,
but he lets her go again without answering.
He wonders if Edyth has told her, and he
hopes in a bored sort of way that she hasn't.

At dinner time he dresses himself carefully.
Reg and Edyth sit opposite each other.   The
wind and sun of the morning have left more
than one little freckle upon her face, and the
pink gown she has put on by no means tones
down the color.   She looks hot and embarrassed.

Presently a lady enters with four gentle-men attending her. She has the graceful walk of a princess, and her simple white silk gown is drawn up just below her neck, showing a long white throat. Mrs. Courtney sees her as she enters, and turns her eyes stonily in another direction. General Court-ney opens his mouth to speak, as he sees her, too, but one look at his wife's face is enough. He closes it upon a bit of bluefish and holds his peace.

He thinks that Mrs. Stanley has been ap-proached, but has probably not shown the proper amount of alacrity in accepting the ready offers of friendship of her distant kin. He isn't so very sorry. She looks nice— and then he looks again and sees that one of the men with her is Richard Baylor, and a dim dawning of the truth comes to the general, and he is more devoted than ever to his fish. Edyth sees them, too, but they are at Reginald's back, and he goes on in blessed unconsciousness of it all.

As for Mary, she feels her best. Every man

in the room in the range of whose vision she
has come is looking at her, but it isn't that
which causes Mary's spirits to rise. That is
an old story to her. Dolly is with her, and
Dolly is pretty, and her husband is there with
his calm, pale, indifferent face. All the others
are like moving shadows to Mary, in the light
of the presence of these two.

And then Mary sees the hostility which has
gone out of its way to haul up its flag against
her. She looks at the men with her, Poncet
and the other two, old acquaintances, elegant
looking men, both of them. She sees that
Reg is eating his dinner and has not seen her,
and that his womenkind do not mean that he
shall. Perhaps Mary would not be a woman
if there was not a little resolve born in that
instant.

Poncet lifts his eyeglass and follows the
direction of Mary's eyes. Then he looks back
at her. Old worldling that he is, he looks at
Baylor, and wonders if a man like that can
always hold the passionate, tempestuous heart
of a woman so much younger than himself,

and he looks at Reg. He glances several times at Edyth, but there is no opening into which he can wedge a question about her, and Poncet learned long ago that it is always safe to let somebody else introduce a personal topic of conversation. One never knows what ground one may be stepping upon.

As soon as possible Mrs. Courtney leads her group up stairs. It is stupider sitting about in a little stuffy room that is a parlor only by courtesy, than strolling off on the verandas or the board walk, but Mrs. Courtney made some murmurs about " objectionable people " and drew down the blinds.

"Edyth," Reg said suddenly, " let's go out and sit in the pavilion. The tide is coming in. It is hot here ;" and Edyth, with her face alight, followed him.

There is an old saying that in every marriage or engagement one of the pair is booted and spurred and the other saddled and bridled. There is none of the self confidence of the conqueror about Reg, but certainly there is none of the meekness of the slave. That rôle,

if it must be played, has been cast for another.
Edyth walks stiffly by her lover's side through
the crowds on the veranda, and then she slips
her hand under his arm. She looks at all the
men they meet and thinks how big and handsome and dear Reg is. He was only civil to
Mrs. Baylor. A man—a gentleman—must be
civil to a woman who literally throws herself
at his head; but he has forgotten all about her
now. They sit down over by the rail where
the waves dash in gloriously and the wind
sweeps boldly.

"May I smoke?"

"Why, yes, of course," Edyth says.

Reg has been smoking in her face ever since
he came home from school with the accomp-
lishment, and some way this request seems to
set her apart from the sisterly rôle she has
always played, and while it puts her away in
a certain sense, draws her nearer, too. It
thrills the heart that has never known any
really thrilling experience. She made little
pictures, air castles, day dreams.

Poor Edyth! They sat there for an hour,

almost silent. Now and then there was something, an extra gust of wind, a passing steamer,
that called out a remark; and then the band
for the dance began to tune up and send out a
bar or two of waltz music. It isn't exactly a
propitious time for Edyth to become playful
and take a sweetheart's privilege of scolding.
But tact is like beauty, reserved for nature's
pets.

"I'm afraid mamma has a rod in pickle for
you, Reg," she says.

"Eh?"

"For staying with Mrs. Baylor and walking
home with her. You know it's altogether
likely that she isn't going to be taken up at
all, down in Ellenbro', and our connection
with her is likely to be embarrassing. *I* think
she *looks* theatrical, don't you?"

"I really didn't notice. It's too cold here
for you; let's go in."

He fairly hurries her up the steps and into
his mother's presence, and then he starts away.
She stops him at the door.

"Where are you going?"

"Oh, nowhere! I'm tired. I'm going to
my room for a while."

"Oh!"

Edyth goes to hers and leans out into the
moonlight. She hardly misses her lover, she
has so much to think about. There is a constant procession on its way to the ball room
across the court. She idly notices some of
them. A beautiful woman, tall, with her silk
train gathered up and a big bunch of pink
roses in her hand, comes out, and—— Edyth
gives a gasp. In evening dress, with radiant
face, dancing attendance, is *Reg*, her Reg, and
the woman is Mrs. Richard Baylor. Edyth
slams the window and goes to bed, her heart
one ache and tears of rage on her pillow.

IV.

MRS. BAYLOR and her party were not
long in following Mrs. Courtney out of
the dining room. She had things to say to
her husband, and she dismissed the men who
hung about her with the cheerful remark that
she was going up stairs to sing Dolly to "bye
low," as was her nightly habit. She mingled
that maternal announcement with promises to
dance at the hop later in the evening. They
may have expected Baylor to go with them,
but his wife held his arm with a determination
that would have done credit to Mrs. Courtney
herself. When Mary wanted her husband
merely because she loved him and couldn't
bear him out of her sight, that was one thing.
Then it was that she charmed him until he saw
no one but her, and she would not have had
him follow her under other conditions; but
when it was a matter of business she kept him

as a right.   Mary had had few whims which
her husband had not indulged her in these
four years.

When they have reached their own apartment
at last, Mary turns around and kisses her husband with her two hands on his shoulders.
He looks into her face, and puts his arm
around her and says, "I just love you, Polly!"
but it is more with the cheerful, off hand air
of saying "It's a fine morning" than with
the ardor of a lover.   Impulsive, impetuous,
spirited Mary wonders sometimes if he does
love her at all, and then she puts her head
against his and passionately declares to herself
that she does not care.   He is hers.

"I have something to tell you: I met all
the Courtneys from down in Ellenbro' this
morning."

"You did?"

"Yes; I went out to swim, you know.   I
didn't know when we first came out that the
young man who saved Dolly's life was young
Courtney that you told me about this morning.   They took me for somebody else and

were very civil to me, and then—don't say
anything to me, Dick, about good manners!
When that old woman whose gown is so tight
it is ready to crack from her back, and that
pasty young woman, found out who I was
they walked off with rudeness—I never saw
anything like it! I suppose that is the sort of
sophisticated mother you think Dolly ought to
have to teach her how to behave and whom
to associate with. Ladies!" and Mrs. Baylor's
scorn was an effect that would have made her
fortune on the stage.

"And how did the young man act?" Mr.
Baylor feels as sure as he ever felt in his life
that Mary has left none of her social debts
lying about for him to pay. He is too indolent to care about most things, but a slight to
his wife in which she had come off second
best would probably find him coming up as a
reinforcement.

"He? He was charming. He stayed and
walked home with me in their faces, and I
have promised dances to him tonight. I hope
those horrors will be there, because I am going

to wear my best gown." She goes down into
her trunk and brings it up. "I'm glad it's
pink. That horribly ugly girl has on a pink
gown, but it looks like a hollyhock by the
side of a tea rose in comparison to mine. But
pshaw!" Mary took her pretty gown and
threw it over the foot of the bed. "Why
should I waste any ammunition on that affair?
That nice boy isn't going to tie himself to a
frump. He has too much appreciation of a
good thing when he sees it," and Mrs. Baylor
looks at herself complacently in the glass.

"You seem to have like powers of recognition," her husband says, an expression which
comes as near a smile as he ever allows himself crossing his pale, taciturn face.

"I have," but as she says it it is at her husband instead of at her own image that Mary
looks.

But even though Mary puts down the
"beauty gown" as too precious to be wasted
upon Atlantic City, she is a beautiful woman
when she enters the ball room, and every man
and woman there turn to look at her. After all

these years she still has too good a walk and a
too evidently studied carriage not to be re-
garded as a little different from other women.
There is that indefinable something about
Mary that seems " profession," that thing that
is the bugbear of most women.

Reginald sees her in the midst of everything
as he comes in. Her husband is hanging
about in the background ; or at least it would
be hanging in the background for any other
man ; but Richard Baylor is something like
MacGregor : where he sits is the head of the
table. He and his wife seem to make back-
grounds of other people.

Looking at Mary one may be sure that she
would have been a star actress. After all it is
personality and charm that makes one actor
different from another, whether it is on the
stage of the world or the stage of a theater.
It isn't that one feels the part more than
another, or even expresses it better. It is the
person who seems to do a thing in the way
we should like to have done it.

But the women may sit and ask their hus-

bands and each other if they know who the
" actress looking woman " is ; there are men
in plenty who want to ask her to dance.   Reg
has hardly the courage to approach her.   She
sees him in a moment and beckons to him to
come to her, her lips parting over her pretty
white teeth.   Courtney hasn't been beckoned
to much ; he feels it all over him, and he goes
over at once.   The question that Mary asks
him isn't exactly what he expects to hear.

" Where are your mother and Miss Smith ? "

" They ?   Oh !   they—they didn't care to
come.   What—dance is mine ? "

Mary hasn't a program.   None of the women
has one.   She has promised to dance the
" next waltz " with half a dozen people.   Only
a minute before she had turned and looked
half wistfully into her husband's face, hoping
he was going to ask her to dance it with him,
but he stays on the outer rim.   Dancing has
lost its savor to Richard Baylor these half a
dozen years, except for that brief interval
when he would have done anything to take
Mary away from another man even for five

minutes. She belongs to him now, for good and all. So Reg seems as good as anybody, lacking Dick, and she says, "Now," as the music comes softly in well timed cadences, and they start off together.

It seems to Reg that never in all his life has he ever danced before. They are dancing in the dining room, from which the chairs and tables have been hastily removed, but to Reg the floor is perfect. Mary decides, as she goes around with him, that he has the making of a good dancer, but the hour hasn't struck which makes him perfect. She thinks longingly of Dick and how he can dance, and looks over Reg's shoulder to see if he is anywhere near.

To Reg there is nothing left. Life has culminated in this hour when Mary Baylor is floating around the room in his arms. He wonders how it has happened that he has never known a woman like this before. He has never believed that they lived except in a story writer's imagination. His eyes fall down upon the little curls about her white nape, and he looks at the firm roundness of her neck and gets a little dizzy.

Mary stops. "Do you know I believe I will go and have an ice?" and tucks her hand under his arm and goes out across the piazza to a little room where people are drinking the mildest of lemon sherbets out of little glass cups. If there is wine to be drunk it is not set out in public.

Mary looks about for her husband, not anxiously, because she is never anxious with the terrors which beset some wives. Baylor has never done anything yet which has disturbed his wife in the least. She knew his habits when she married him, and he has always gone about his affairs in a way which precluded any idea that he might possibly be criticised. When she sees that he has gone and that Poncet and the other men have also disappeared, the reason is perfectly apparent to her. She knows that up stairs in her parlor, of which she has just taken possession, there is in progress a game in which disks of ivory in red and white and blue are playing a very prominent part.

" They have all gone off and left me," she
says. " I don't see what there is for you to do
but take care of me." It is at this instant that
Edyth looks out of her bed room window and
sees them. Mary looks in upon the dancing
again. There aren't many people in the ball
room. None that she seems to care anything
about. She wonders what she came for; the
light of it all has gone out.

" Come along," she says. " Let us go up
to my little parlor and we will see what they
are all doing. That husband of mine is certain to be led into mischief, and I am afraid
they've left the doors open into Dolly's room,
and the poor child will be suffocated by smoke."

Reg follows her obediently enough. There
is a cloud of smoke already circling toward the
ceiling. They do not even enter the room.
Mary slips softly into the other chamber and
closes the door between it and Dolly, and then
comes back to Reg. There is a little balcony
outside, and they steal out there and sit in the
white light of the moon. The honeysuckle,
yellow and white, which the sea air seems to

foster, grows up almost to their hand and lavishes its sweetness upon the soft air blowing in from the ocean.

Reg has forgotten that there lives on the earth another than the beautiful woman beside him.   He feels ten years older and in another world.   Mary tries to hear the words inside, the words of the game, whose meaning she knows so well, to tell her whether her husband is losing or winning.   She does not want him to lose, because when he does he is just a little quieter and more sarcastic.

" You will find Ellenbro' very different from all this, Mrs. Baylor."

" What *this ?* "

" Oh, the sea and the gaiety."

" I suppose from the way your mother and cousin treated me today that whatever gaiety there is I shall not share in."   Of course it is neither courteous nor tactful for Mary to say any such thing, but there is a plaintive little note in her voice which robs it of its discourtesy, and it touches Reg as she perhaps understands that it will.

His face flushes and his voice takes on a note of deep embarrassment. "My mother did not understand."

"Oh, yes, she did—only too well. I know exactly how they all mean to treat me down there. I am a Bohemian, born into all the heritages of that race. I know what to expect now. I can understand, as though I had inherited that knowledge, too. My mother was a dancer, Mr. Courtney; I wonder if the Ellenbro' people know that? She was a pretty, gay, light hearted woman who married a man who broke her heart. Mr. Poncet knew him. When I was going to marry Dick he came and told me about it as a warning. He thinks stage people ought to marry people of their own sort. But it seemed to me that Dick was just exactly my sort. I don't know anybody who is more of a Bohemian than he is."

Reginald does not want to talk about Mrs. Baylor's husband.

"Where did you live when you were a child?" He could imagine what a pretty, gay little thing she must have been.

"In Paris. My mother was an American, though. My sister and I—we were almost the same age—but this cannot interest you." Mary suddenly remembers that Dick never cares to hear about those old days—and there are some memories which she has brought up which make her own voice tremulous—memories that are the only break in her happy life, she thinks.

"It interests me very much. I have lived so quietly. I know almost nothing of the world."

"Oh, that's delightful!" Mary says cheerfully. "You will learn. I have never had a friend who did not know too much of the world. All you ought to know I will teach you. We are going to be friends, aren't we?"

"It is all yours to say," Reg replies happily. He almost hopes Ellenbro' will not come in a body to call at Castle Hill. He sees himself daily walking with Dolly and her mother about the old paths.

It is twelve o'clock when Mary gets up to go inside and Reg must tear himself away.

It seems as though it must be only nine. As he slips along the corridor and pushes his large and blatant key into his lock, his mother's room door opens and she stands there in a bed room wrapper with a Bible in her hand, and with every air of having just read of the sharpness of having a thankless child.

"Reginald," she says, "where have you been?"

"I?" He looks his stubbornest. "I have been spending a very charming evening with Mrs. Baylor on her balcony."

And then they shut their respective doors.

VII.

MRS. STANLEY was a woman of the world beyond all things. The position that she had made for herself in society showed to advantage the adaptability of the American girl. Brought up in a country town, she had early married a young lieutenant in the army and had managed, by an exercise of her wit and good humor and likableness, to keep her husband at the best Eastern stations. He was a colonel now, all by reason of his wife's admirable way of turning trumps and playing the small cards in her hand to the best advantage.

It was popularly supposed that she had come down to Atlantic City for the wonderful tonic there is in the air and to obtain rest from the onerous social duties which surrounded her in Washington and New York. But Mrs. Stanley knew better. There was a coveted position that was going to be empty in a few months, and which it seemed to her had been created especially that her big, handsome husband might fill it. There was a Cabinet officer who was given over to good works and whose very democratic tastes led him to Atlantic City for the summer. It had seemed to Mrs. Stanley a very propitious time for cultivating his acquaintance. A man is much likelier to give an appointment to a man he likes and whose wife he likes than to an utter stranger.

Mrs. Stanley feared that the great man might think her frivolous from the stories that he had heard of her. It seemed a good time to teach him better. There were seaside charities in which a woman might interest herself, and Mrs. Stanley speedily discovered which was the object of the Cabinet minister's solicitude, and devoted herself to that. They were in need of money. The Cabinet minister was very rich, and Mrs. Stanley was not exactly poverty stricken, but an entertainment would attract attention and possible contributions with much more success than the simple drawing of a check, thus keeping the left hand

from a knowledge of the right hand's good
works.

It was the morning after the dance that
Mrs. Stanley sat over her breakfast table and
pondered. Mrs. Stanley had no children, and
the little table that held the china and silver
was dainty and bright with flowers, and over
it with the aroma of the coffee there hung that
air of confidence that always comes when a
man thinks his wife is the cleverest woman in
the world.

Mrs. Stanley was forty, but in her girlish duck
linen gown and sailor hat nobody would take
her to be past twenty five. She was arrayed
this morning for going out. Her white silk
umbrella and white gloves lay on a chair
beside her, and her big, loose white veil was
all ready to adjust.

"Yes," she was saying as she broke a lump
of sugar in two that Colonel Stanley's coffee
might be sweetened exactly to his taste, "I
am going up to the hotel where the Honorable
Jacob is staying and get up some sort of an
entertainment. I can find somebody, I suppose.

The Honorable Jacob owns property in
this part of the country and he likes to see
'the quality' disporting themselves in the
neighborhood."

"Where are you going to get your talent?"
The colonel is good natured and passive. He
considers his wife a creator; that she has only
to say, "Let it be," and it is. But sometimes
her methods amuse him.

"Oh, I am going up to the hotel. When I
went into the hop last night I heard two or
three men speak of a very pretty 'actressy'
woman. She seemed to be somebody who was
not unmentionable from the way they spoke.
I couldn't get much information out of them,
but enough to make me think that I might
find my *pièce de résistance* right there. It
would be a good advertisement for the hotel
for them to let us have theatricals in the
dining room, especially as the Honorable Jacob
will attend. Oh, I can arrange it all. I found
out last night that I have some kin, some
of my sixtieth cousins from down in Ellenbro',
over there at the hotel. It appears that the

pretty actress' husband is an Ellenbro' man.
Maybe another connection of mine, for all I
know. I've got a branch of my family tree
budding into that of almost every other Southern stalk. At any rate I am going over to the
hotel and see what I can drum up. The
Honorable Jacob looks with favor upon anything which will assist him to be conspicuous
as a man of charity and not bear upon his
purse." And after breakfast Mrs. Stanley ad-
justed her veil, spread her white parasol, and
took her departure.

An hour later Mrs. Courtney and Edyth
were sitting on the shady corner of the piazza.
Reg had gone up the board walk to buy some
trifle for his mother. Mrs. Courtney had gazed
rather charily upon the slender, white clad figure
that had come up the steps and gone into the
office. After her experiences of the day before
she looked every strange woman over critically,
and it seemed to her that there were not only
flaws, but radical faults which would condemn
them to the unvisited state, in each. So when
the white duck gown and sailor hat made a

second appearance and walked straight up to her, she received it with a stoniness of mien which would have overawed almost anybody but Mrs. Stanley. That calm woman held out a hand with an unabated cordiality.

"It is Mrs. Courtney from Ellenbro', isn't it? I wonder if you have forgotten that there is such a person as Helen Stanley—Helen Lacy?"

"Indeed I have not." Mrs. Courtney rises with the smile which had been so cruelly nipped in the bud yesterday. This is a great deal better than she had hoped for. She introduces Edyth to Mrs. Stanley, and they all sit down to talk. Mrs. Stanley takes in poor Edyth. She had heard of her, and she had vaguely hoped to find some material here for this scheme of entertainment which she has on hand. She had expected to find her pretty, at any rate. Beauty is supposed to be the birthright of a girl born south of Mason and Dixon's line, but Edyth did not meet approval in Mrs. Stanley's eyes. She looked to her like a libel upon the South, whose fame as a mother of beautiful and tactful women she herself had done so much to keep up. Mrs. Courtney struck her as frumpier than the frumpiest, with none of the sweetness and motherliness which she had expected.

By the time she had talked to them ten minutes, she wondered what she had hunted them up for. There only remained the possible hope of their introducing the pretty woman she had heard of. But Mrs. Stanley had doubts even of this. The Courtneys did not look like people who would be likely to be intimate with any " pretty actressy woman." But she put on her pleasantest voice, and asked :

" Were you at the dance last night ? " She had turned to Edyth. " I do not remember seeing you there ! "

" I do not approve of these mixed dances at seaside places at all," Mrs. Courtney said stiffly. " You are apt to meet such a curious crowd. So different from the people one is accustomed to."

" Yes "—Mrs. Stanley's smile was bland—

"that is true. But do you know, it is rather
upon that account that I like them. You see
people that you see nowhere else. Aren't
you inclined to find all sorts of originalities
among the men and women who are not bound
by conventionalities? Aren't they an interesting study to you?" Her large, soft bright
eyes went from one face to the other. There
was a little lightening in Edyth's face. She
had thought that some way and somehow it
might be pleasant to go off with Reg if she
knew exactly how, and see and do things that
were unheard of in Ellenbro'. But Edyth's
face was not expressive enough for Mrs. Stanley to catch the glow. She only saw the look
of stony disapproval in Mrs. Courtney's eyes,
and I am afraid Mrs. Stanley's tact left her
and she felt the joy that comes at times to
even the best of us, of shocking those who
would sit in judgment.

"I think that is one of the advantages of a
small town. There everybody knows everybody else, and when there are people who break
away from the ordinary bounds you all are able

to study their tricks and manners. Now, in a large city, everybody whom it is possible for you to know is cut on exactly the same pattern."

"A very good pattern cannot be used too often," Mrs. Courtney said, with the air of having invented a proverb.

"True enough, but the same thing over and over does become a little tiresome now and then;" and then Mrs. Stanley prepared to ask about Mary Baylor. But at that instant Reg came up the steps. His mother beckoned and he walked over to them.

Mrs. Stanley looked him over in the second of his approaching and decided that he was the redeeming feature of the family. Mrs. Stanley had not been living among men for twenty years not to know the good, sound specimens when she saw them.

She stood up and shook hands with Reginald very heartily. She liked young men, and they, appreciating her friendship and the good time she gave them, liked her.

"You are just the person I am looking for, my young cousin," she said gaily. "I am trying to get up a little play, some tableaux, what not." She threw out her hands to express her willingness to entertain in any way. "And I am looking for a prince for my fairy tale. Will you be it?"

"A prince in a fairy tale? Well, I am afraid that is hardly a natural rôle," Reg began. He was not learned in the light answers to light speeches.

"Oh, well, actors all say that it is the rôle which is entirely foreign to their natures which they do best. All this is for sweet charity's sake. I know your mother will approve."

"What is it?" Mrs. Courtney asked.

"The Seaside Home for Shop Girls. We think it a very fine charity. The Honorable Jacob Leland, the Cabinet member, is very actively interested in it, and has enlisted my sympathies. They send down two shop girls from each store at a time, and give them a week's outing. We want to get up an entertainment to bring in some much needed funds. I had thought of theatricals."

"Of course Reginald will do everything in

his power to assist you," Mrs. Courtney said.
"And so will Edyth. It will be delightful.
A little play seems to be just the thing."

"I am glad you like the idea. It pleases
me. Some gay, sparkling little comedy. Something short and brisk."

"But I have had absolutely no experience,"
Reg begins.

"That's not of the least consequence," Mrs.
Stanley says, with that air of taking possession
which most young men find perfectly irresistible in an older woman, and particularly an
older woman who looks as much like a younger
woman as Mrs. Stanley does. But as he looks
at her and admires her, leaning over the back
of a chair and facing him, with that look
which your truly successful conquering woman
never loses out of her eyes, whatever her age,
he laughs at the idea of pretty, jolly, girlish,
round cheeked Mary Baylor having been taken
for Mrs. Stanley. Mrs. Stanley was charming,
but to Reg's eyes she was not young.

"By the by," the mistress of the contemplated revels continues, "I have been hearing something about a townswoman of yours who is here, who I fancy may be of enormous assistance to us. They say she is so pretty and has such an air. Two or three gentlemen spoke to me of her last night. I didn't come in until late, and it seems she only stayed a few minutes. Nobody seemed to know much about her, but I gathered enough to know she could probably help us out."

It seemed that Mrs. Stanley was never to be allowed to finish her sentences, which were to culminate with the dreadful fact that she wanted to know Mary Baylor. General Courtney now added his personality to the group.

He was genuinely glad to see Helen Lacy. He knew family histories that precious few people cared to hear talked about nowadays. Neither did Mrs. Stanley care if he had but known it, but he could not believe that, when so much of it concerned her own immediate ancestry. And as long as Mrs. Stanley had nothing better to do than to listen to his reminiscences, the general would never be likely to discover it.

There were greetings to be made, and then they all seemed to settle into the cordial talk of old friends, old friends from home. Finally the conversation led back to Mrs. Stanley's desire to have Reg help her with theatricals. She stopped suddenly in the midst of her talk.

"I cannot imagine who it can be of whom you are speaking," Mrs. Courtney said. "I do not know of any of our Ellenbro' girls who are here—except Edyth, and she——" Mrs. Courtney looked at her as though she might have left behind her a buzz of talk at the hop last night if she had only had the foresight to go—"was not at the dance. I know that if any of them had been here they would naturally have sought us out at once. There are plenty of charming girls in Ellenbro'."

"I think this young woman coming must be the one I am in search of," Mrs. Stanley said, looking with eyes which could look with amused sympathy upon another woman being adored. "I am sure from the description that this must be she."

Reg looked, and it seemed to him that woman

was fickle and woman was vain. Two or
three of the men of the night before had managed to meet Baylor and be introduced to his
wife, and Mary was strolling slowly home from
her morning bath attended by no less than
three, counting Poncet.

"That must be the Mrs. Baylor they mentioned," Mrs. Stanley said. "Isn't her husband
one of our numerous connections? She is
exactly the person to help with those theatricals. I want to ask you to introduce us."

Mrs. Courtney cleared her throat. "I cannot say that I consider Mrs. Baylor an acquaintance. Nor——" but Reg stepped in. "I
know her very well, Mrs. Stanley. I should
be glad to introduce you."

Our boy was getting independent. Mrs.
Stanley rose quickly to get out of the impend-
ing storm, and Reg followed her. Mary saw
them coming, and the faces they had left behind. If she had had any doubt before, she
knew now, that it was to be war between her
and Mrs. Courtney. She held out her hand
smilingly to Reg.

There was a calm dignity in Reg's face
which set well upon his rather rugged and
manly features and frame. Reg was only an
inexperienced youth, but he had in a measure
been forced into contact with Mrs. Baylor, and
he was enjoying his acquaintance with her as
he had never enjoyed anything in his not too
gaily colored life.

He took her hand now with every sign of
pleasure in seeing her again, and stepping to
one side said, "Allow me to introduce you to
my cousin, Mrs. Stanley, who has expressed a
wish to know you, Mrs. Baylor."

Mrs. Stanley's face was smiles and her hand
was out. The men about Mrs. Baylor had
withdrawn into the background; Poncet's eyes
were on the horizon.

"I fancy we might find that we were relatives, too," Mrs. Stanley said. Mrs. Courtney
gave a sort of gasp. This was going it. But
Mrs. Stanley was not a woman to do things by
halves. When she started out she took her
largest ammunition along with her. She never
made the sorry mistake of patronizing the

people she wanted anything from, nor the one as equally serious, of giving them the impression that she was trying to get something to her own advantage. There is a surface honesty of speech which appeals to all of us, and Mrs. Stanley was a past mistress in its art.

"I believe I am related to half the people in the South, and I suppose the Baylors are likely to be in my line of kin. Any way, Mrs. Baylor, I hope you have Southern feeling enough to help me out—kin or no kin—with a little project of mine."

The cordial face and hearty hand were too much for Mary. It was what she had hoped might come to her in the home she was going to, and it warmed her heart.

"I hardly know what I can do," she said, smiling back, "but it shall be what I can."

"We are going to try to get up an entertainment for the Shop Girls' Seaside Home. We want to give a little play, just some sparkling little comedy. Say for two." And she looked at Reg and then back to Mary. "'Half an Hour Under an Umbrella,' or 'A Morning

Ride,' or something of that sort. Don't you think you could help me?"

"I'm sure——" began Mary, and then a little cloud came over the brilliant, mobile face; the thought of Richard and what he would say. He hated any reference to her stage life. He never had said so—she could not remember that he had ever said so, but she felt it. The bored expression that was habitual to his quiet, fair face was accented when the old days were mentioned. To Mary the thought of again feeling the pulse of an audience was like the strongest stimulant. But all this she had left to become Richard Baylor's wife, and first and foremost he was always in her heart.

"I must first ask my husband what his plans are," she went on very prettily. It seemed so pretty and so good that Mrs. Courtney rather resented it. She was not anxious that Reg should see anything which she herself would admire in Mrs. Baylor. Everything was going away from Mrs. Courtney's road any way. There was a dryness in her throat and a burn-

ing in her breast which was virtuous indignation. That this creature should be encouraged!

"Your husband, of course," Mrs. Stanley
said. "But husbands are easily managed. I
fancy you will not have much difficulty."

Mary smiled a vague little smile and went
up stairs with a promise to send Mrs. Stanley
a note later in the day.

"The idea of that pretty woman not manag-
ing her husband!" Mrs. Stanley said, laughing, as she turned back.

"Manage him! Of course." Mrs. Courtney's voice was full of scorn. "Didn't she
manage him into marrying her? Pardon me,
Helen," and there was a decided chill in the
tones, "but I think you are making a great, a
serious mistake in giving Richard Baylor's
wife so prominent a place in your entertainment. He is a man who is by no means in
good odor—a black sheep, in fact; a man who
has made a precarious living about newspaper
offices, and his wife has been an actress."

"An actress! Has she really? If that
isn't fortunate!"

Mrs. Stanley's eyes were bright.

"Why didn't you tell me that in the beginning? She must select her own play."

Mrs. Courtney retired into offended silence. She did not even say that Ellenbro' would certainly not receive Mrs. Baylor. The events of the last few hours had settled that in her mind once and forever.

Mary went slowly up the wide, uncarpeted steps of the summer hotel. She knew that her husband was lying on the lounge in their parlor with a brandy and soda at his elbow, and a pile of newspapers and a new book or two adjacent. It is a little habit which Mary has kept all through these years to run over to her husband when she comes in and let him know that she is there, if it is only by a little squeeze of his arm. It is an attention that he takes, as he does everything else in life, with good natured indifference. But she does not go at once now. She steps to the mirror and takes her hatpins out carefully, one by one, and ruffles up her bangs, watching his face as she does it.

If he had only arisen and come over to her with that little caress, Mary's heart would have been full. But she does not expect it of him, and his eyes never leave his paper. He knows that she will be perched somewhere about the sofa in a minute or two, and he can wait. There is none of the impatience of life about Richard Baylor.

"I met a lady from the South just now. She said you might be a cousin of hers. She was a Mrs. Stanley."

"Did you?" Mr. Baylor says indifferently. "Was she nice?"

"Yes, she was. She is getting up a charity entertainment for something. I didn't listen to the cause. I think it was something about shop girls—and she wants me—she has asked me—to take part—to act."

Mr. Baylor hardly moves his paper.

"And are you going to do it?"

"I told her I would ask you."

"Oh, do as you like."

If Mr. Baylor could see in the glass he would note a little tear start from Mary's long lashes and go down her cheek, but his paper holds him again. Mary does not go to his side. She walks over to the desk by one of her windows and writes a little note. After it is finished she sits facing out upon the sea, a pensive look upon her face, a face that was not made for pensive looks, but for gaiety and smiles. Baylor looks up and sees the unfamiliar shadow. It does not please him to see shadows anywhere. The sun must shine in his world.

"What are you going to play and where is it to be?" he asks.

"I——" There is confusion and then a light in her face. "I have just written to decline. I—thought you wouldn't care to have me."

"By all means," Baylor says with conviction. He isn't particularly anxious to recall to the world, and it will be recalling it to all their new world if Mary takes this part while the Courtneys are here, that his wife was taken from the stage door. But in his heart Baylor cares little for the world beyond his own immediate surroundings. He has married his wife without considering his world, and now she—and himself—shall not be made unhappy by any such tardy consideration.

"Do you truly mean it? Oh, Dick, you *darling!*" and she rushes over to him and puts her young arms about his neck and her fresh, fair, smooth cheek to his rather worn one, worn a little more today than it was yesterday.

"I see no reason why you should not accept Mrs. Stanley's invitation. It will probably be a stupid event, as events go, but you like to meet new people, and you like—to act. Yes, I should say accept by all means."

Mary took the note she had written and dramatically tore it to bits. Mrs. Courtney would have said that it was another sign of her shiftless breeding that the scraps of paper went floating over the carpet and were allowed to remain there.

"Dick—boy, you are a darling!" and she danced back to the desk and wrote Mrs. Stanley an enthusiastic note of acceptance, a note which caused that lady to lift up a sigh of relief that so much burden was off her mind.

VIII.

AROUND Mrs. Stanley's brightly lighted dinner table sit the Honorable Jacob, drinking his claret and champagne with the same air of not knowing what he is doing with which he eats his soup and breaks his bread ; Mr. and Mrs. Baylor, and Reg. It isn't often that Mrs. Stanley pays another woman the compliment of being her single feminine companion at a dinner table, but she has rightly judged that Mary would be quite equal to the occasion. Men, in however great numbers, have no terrors for Mrs. Baylor, and awe of a great position she knows not. One man is very much like another in her eyes, always excepting her husband.

To Mrs. Stanley's surprise, she finds Richard Baylor delightful. He can talk and he does talk remarkably well. He looks well at the table. There is an air of exquisite gentlemanliness about him, the finish of the true cosmopolitan.

The Honorable Jacob has expressed his entire approval of the project of the theatricals.

"We have not decided upon a play as yet. We are going to leave that to Mrs. Baylor's experience," Mrs. Stanley says.

"But I know nothing of amateur plays——" Mary begins. Mrs. Stanley's husband looks at her. He never interferes, easy as it would be for him to change the subject, by a quick question. Nor does Mrs. Stanley. She desires it understood that she is entertaining Mrs. Baylor professionally.

"What sort do you know about?" the ponderous Jacob asks, with a playful smile. He is thinking that you can tell a country girl wherever you see her. This combination of beauty and simplicity could only have come from Ellenbro'. He knows Ellenbro'. He has a railroad and a big farm and a place where he goes to hunt down in that part of the country.

"Oh, the real ones. I was an actress, or educated for an actress, before I married."

Mr. Leland looks at her hard, and then he says, "Did you like it? It's a hard life, isn't it?"

"Oh, I suppose, to people who have been brought up differently, but to me—— Oh, when I hear people saying it is a hard life, I always think of that poor old French actress who, when she was dying, confessed to the priest. When he gave her absolution, he said, 'My poor daughter! What a miserable life yours has been!' And she began to cry, saying, 'What happy times those were when I was so miserable!' I am like that about my acting." She has forgotten everything; has forgotten that her husband does not like to hear of those old days, and her eyes are bright.

"An honest little woman, by Jove!" the big colonel thinks.

The Honorable Jacob looks at her and smiles, while Richard Baylor idly twists his wine glass round and round, and Reg's face flushes a little.

There isn't much learned talk. Usually

when the Honorable Mr. Leland goes out to dinner the subjects are ponderous. He thinks, as he says good by to his hostess, that he never has had so pleasant an evening, and he tells her so. She sees in his eyes that she may ask him to dinner in Washington in the fall; that they are going to be friends; and she thanks Mrs. Baylor, and makes up her mind that while they are down here, and these theatricals are going on, and there will be no consequences to follow, she will be extra civil to her.

The colonel and Mr. Baylor linger in the veranda with their cigars.

"You are not going to smoke, my young cousin," Mrs. Stanley says. It is time for everybody to go home, but Richard Baylor and Mary are so unaccustomed to civilized ways that it seems early in the evening to them, and the example of the great man no precedent for any course of conduct. "You and Mrs. Baylor are going to talk about a play. What *shall* it be? It must be something short and pretty." Mary has been thinking.

"I know a play," she says, "that I think we might get. It was written for a 'curtain raiser' by a young artist I know, and has only been played once to a houseful of critics. They were enthusiastic in its praise. It is short, and there are only four characters. It is a seashore play, too." A dreamy look came into her eyes. "It is a very lovely, touching little story," she added quietly.

"What is it like? What are the characters?" Mrs. Stanley was looking at her, wondering why she had not been clever enough to go on with her stage career. There was where she belonged. There was where she fitted in. That was the life for her.

"It is called 'Alice.' It opens on a light-house during a storm, or just after a storm. A boat containing a beautiful young woman has been dashed ashore, and she is taken up by the light keeper, cared for by his old mother and his sweetheart. The light keeper falls in love with her. She is a stranger from another world to him, a thing to be worshiped; a gentle, tender thing to be cared for. To the

woman—to Alice—this simple place is a haven
of rest. She wants to stay there forever, but
she sees that she has brought discord into the
house, and she goes, first telling them her sad
story."

" And that ? "

"Oh, you must read the play. I cannot
tell it. Telling stories is not my gift."

" I should think it might be," Mrs. Stanley
says warmly.

Mary has been sitting on the piano stool,
her bare, round white arm laid along the ivory
keys, which look old and yellow beside the
pink life of her flesh. There is a lamp with
a red shade behind her dark head. Reg leans
over the end of the piano, never knowing,
poor boy, how much he is showing in his face.

Mrs. Stanley is thinking.

" Who could do the other characters? Are
they difficult ? "

" Which are the others ? "

" Of course you will do *Alice* and Mr. Courtney, my young cousin, Reginald here, will be
the light keeper."

Mary nods approvingly. She can see Reg as the *Nat* of the play already. She looks at him judicially. There is no possible self consciousness in her. She sees only the possible actor. Reg would hardly be flattered could he know that as she looks at him she sees his dress changed to the rough clothing of the young light keeper, and that she is thinking that he will look the part, and after all, for such an entertainment as this, that is the principal thing. Amateurs are not expected to act by any one except their nearest friends, and they are always supposed by them to have succeeded. To Mary's mind, educated professionally, the amateur is very funny, but she is too politely tactful to say so. And she herself has been away from it all so long that she feels doubtful of her own powers.

"The character of the mother of the light keeper is a beautiful one. A plain, sweet tempered, simple and yet wise woman. A character that deserves careful study. I should like to try that myself."

"But you are to be *Alice*. I wonder——"

Mrs. Stanley put her teeth upon her lower lip and let her eyes gaze into vacancy, while she thought. "M—m—I'll send for her tomorrow. I *think* I know some one who could do that part."

"Your cousin could play the sweetheart," Mary says, looking at Reg. His face has been burning a little with excitement all the evening. There is a look in his eyes and an expression about his mouth that is new born. It is incipent intoxication, caused by a stimulant more insidious than alcohol. At the mention of Edyth the color goes deeper.

"My cousin has had no experience." He wonders if Mary is trying to bring Edyth into the play through any motive of revenge, and then as he looks into her candid, interested eyes, he shames himself for the thought. There is no lack of generosity here. And here, too, he begins to have a glimmering sense that there is something beside personalities considered. Here is the mind which sees a person at his true value in any position, irrespective of likes and dislikes.

"I should be glad to coach her. Unless——"
she looks at Mrs. Stanley, "there is some one
else."

Mrs. Stanley is glad to placate Mrs. Courtney by the suggestion of bringing Edyth into
the play. She judges at once that the part is
small and insignificant or Mrs. Baylor would
not have suggested her for it. And so it is
settled.

Baylor and his wife and Reg go home along
the deserted board walk. The moon is making
its most gorgeous glittering pathway across
the sea. The solemnity of the night is over
them all. Baylor is thinking that Colonel
Stanley is a good fellow, and with half
humorous consciousness of his own short-
comings, is telling himself that that is the
sort of man he ought to associate with. It
would be wholesome, but something of a bore.

Mary is dreaming of "Alice." As she looks
at the sea she shudders at its loneliness to one
tossed adrift out there in an open boat, all
alone. She involuntarily grasps her husband's
arm a little tighter. He looks down into her

face and smiles at the wistful expression with
which it is turned up to his. If Reginald
were not there he would kiss her, but making
a sentimental scene is out of the question. It
is Mary who would do a thing like that. He
presses her hand on his sleeve a little closer.

As for Reg, Reg does not know why, but he
is happy.

Mrs. Stanley stands before the mirror in her
bed room and takes the hairpins out of her
hair, and carefully places in its box that por-
tion of it which she keeps for daily wear.

"I tell you," she says to her husband, as she
draws the brush over her locks, "that woman
is making the greatest mistake. What rest-
less, silly things women are any way. Here
are society women, breaking their necks and
the hearts of their families to go on the stage
and make indifferent actresses, and here is a
woman born and brought up in the life, loving
it as she loves nothing else, breaking her own
heart to get into a society too stupid for anybody to stand. We are all like Bluebeard's
wives, pounding ever at the one locked door."

IX.

"YOU ought to know perfectly well that I will not allow Edyth to act in a public hotel with that woman!" Mrs. Courtney feels vicious. "Of course they cannot get along without her, and I knew that Helen Stanley would see that she could not."

Reginald has little sense of humor, and he has so fine an appreciation of Edyth's good qualities that his mother's remark fell upon what would seem to be ears unappreciative of the merits of the situation. Mrs. Stanley would think so.

"The suggestion——" Reginald was going to say that the suggestion came from Mrs. Baylor, but he thought better of that and took his coffee instead. The play had come, brought down by its owner, who was just starting away on his summer holiday when Mrs. Baylor's note reached him; and who,

with the easy adjustment of the artistic tem-
perament, changed his plans in half an hour
and came to Atlantic City instead. He was
not at all anxious that his play should be produced by amateurs, but he was fond of Mrs.
Baylor and ready to be good natured, and as
she herself was to personify the character over
which he had labored, and which he loved, he
was ready to hand it over to her. He was an
aggressive looking young man, with keen blue
eyes, covered by glasses, the rimless, string-
less variety which look as though they had
grown on the face. His hair was parted exactly
in the middle above his rather pale forehead,
with not a hair awry, and his mustache was
cut straight across, as though an end might
disgrace its owner by curling. It was an alert,
firm personality, the very last that would be
expected to hold poetic fancies, tender fancies.
And yet "Alice" seemed to have been dug out
of a woman's heart.

Mrs. Stanley forgot Mrs. Baylor's description of the play as he was introduced to her,
and gave his hand an unconventional grip and

expected a comedy. She had brought along
the young lady who had been sent for to take
the part of the mother. She had been vaguely
chosen because she had taken parts in amateur
plays, and because she was so young and
blooming that she could not possibly be
offended or regard it as other than a lark to
personate an old woman. She looked at Reg
with eyes that were a little inclined toward
audacity when Mrs. Stanley mentioned that he
was to be her son. The rather affected man-
nishness of her dress was accented by her
manner. One expected her to take off her hat
when she came into the room. There was none
of the solemnity which the masculine girl
usually bears about with her, as though she
felt it her duty to uphold the dignity of her
adopted sex. She was rather like a jolly boy.
When Mr. Covert, the playwriting artist, was
introduced to her as " Miss Marshall, the young
lady who is to play the mother," he screwed
up his near sighted eyes without any attempt
to disguise his disgust.

"Don't you think I kin play with yore

doll rags?" she asked with a Yankee drawl that might have come from down East.

His face cleared at once. "You can talk it, any way," he said. "But how in the mischief are you going to *look* it?"

"I'll attend to that. But say, isn't Mrs. Baylor simply gorgeous?"

"That's what she is! You just ought to hear her recite. I wouldn't let this play be acted by anybody else for this sort of thing. I've worked too hard over it, but everything she does to it will make it 'takier.' She's *great!*"

Notwithstanding Mrs. Courtney's protests, Edyth had come with Reg to this morning's reading of the play. She felt that she could not let Reg get as far away from her as he would seem by going into this work and play without her. She was a little stiff and cold, and the merry chatter of talk about the hotel parlor, where they had gathered, left her isolated. She had nothing to say. The talk of her little world was personal and local. This was personal, but it was not local.

The reason the talk of people who travel about and live in a large world, seems so much wider, is because it covers more area. Essentially there is little difference; the habit of thought is practically the same. Cultivation is often only the knowledge to talk about more things.

Mrs. Stanley pounded on the edge of the piano with the stick of her lorgnette.

"We have met here this morning to read a play which we are going to produce here in the hotel for the benefit of the Seaside Home for Shop Girls. The proprietor has kindly offered us the use of the dining room and will arrange a stage and accessories."

"You'll need a kitchen scene," the author of the play announced; "a cook stove, and all that sort of thing."

"No, we won't," Mrs. Stanley replied. "We are going to pretend that the acting is in the sitting room. We can put shells and things from the board walk stores all about."

"Pretend!" And the author sniffed.

"Never mind," Mary whispered. "I'll see that it's all right."

" Mrs. Baylor will read the play."

It was a charming, pathetic little story, and Mary's voice was modulated to each turn of expression.

" My ! " said the girl who had been cast for the mother. " I don't know but it would be a better showing to have Mrs. Baylor take all the parts. I'm awfully glad I came down. I'll learn a lot from her. Who is she, any way ? "

" She was educated for an actress," Covert said, as though he were telling that she was the daughter of a king.

"Oh!" The Philadelphia young woman, notwithstanding her masculine independence and free and easy manners, looked a bit uneasy. " I thought Mrs. Stanley said she belonged to one of the old Southern families."

" Her husband does, and precious little good it does him. She is nothing of the sort."

"I thought——" but the Philadelphia young lady did not tell what she thought. She relapsed into silence.

As the reading went on and on, Edyth's

face took on a deeper and a deeper color. She was not, as Mrs. Stanley imagined, overcome by the impossibility of taking creditably the part assigned her, but she was stiff with self consciousness as she saw how it mirrored her own jealousy in the country girl who daily saw her lover going farther and farther from her in his admiration for the beautiful stranger. The suspicions of the girl in the play, which were afterward verified by Alice's sad story, brought into being ugly ideas in Edyth's own mind ; ideas which she was honest enough to try to put away from her. She looked at Reg. His eyes were upon Mary's face. He was lost in the story, lost in the tones of her voice, and a pang went to Edyth's heart. He was hers, but only as this other girl's lover had been hers.

The story ended, and there were exclamations all over the room. Two or three ladies, who were to assist at the entertainment, had come in, and there was a soft clapping of hands. Mary's face was flushed, too. It all sounded so kind. She knew applause, but this was different. She felt that perhaps after all she was going to like these kind people who belonged to her husband's old life. Dolly was to be brought up in all this. She felt grateful and happy. She forgave Mrs. Courtney—and she turned away from congratulations and plans and went over to the window where Edyth sat in overdressed loneliness.

"Good morning," she said with light hearted gaiety. "Don't you think that as we are all here in the hotel, it would be a good idea to study our parts together? I think you will do *Bessie* capitally."

Edyth turned about with a face that was almost rigid.

"It is impossible for me to take any part in the play."

Mrs. Stanley was just behind. "What *gaucherie!*" she said to herself. "That poor girl might have been brought up with the cows for all the sense she has." Sense to Mrs. Stanley meant social tact.

Mary was chilled for an instant, and then it

looked a little amusing. She turned away.
Reg followed her and never knew when Edyth
went up stairs. The part of *Bessie* was taken
by a young girl in the family where Miss Marshall was visiting. She was not "out" yet,
her mother said, but it was Atlantic City,
where everything was pardonable except being
there—and the cause was a charity. She was
good natured, and like most people found Mrs.
Stanley's pleadings irresistible. All along that
lady had thought Edyth too homely for the part.

"It wants a pretty girl. One cannot forgive
an ugly girl for a mistake."

They rehearsed all day long. The play was
to be produced in five days, and there were
costumes to be prepared. People about the
hotel talked of nothing else, and they looked
upon those who had come since the arrange-
ments were made as decidedly new people,
who had no real part in the festivities.

Reg lived in a regular fever. There was
stiffness and discomfort in his mother's rooms,
but he had an excellent excuse for being there
as little as possible. Often he dined or

lunched, and once even breakfasted, when
they were going to have an early rehearsal and
had all gathered there, at Mrs. Baylor's table.
Twice Mrs. Courtney had announced that they
would leave the next day, but as there was no
response from Reg, she had moved her flitting
on again. One night, coming in late, he had
found Edyth just coming out of their common
parlor into her own room and his heart smote
him. There was no ill temper in her face, but
it looked unhappy.

"Whither away?" he said lightly, and putting his arm about her shoulders drew her back
into the parlor. Reg felt gay. There was
about the sunshine, the sky, the earth, a new
glory. He had thrown himself heart and
soul into the production of the little play.
He laughed at the squabbles of Covert and
Miss Marshall, and he had a brotherly feeling
for the very young and very pretty girl who
had taken the part of *Bessie*, and who had to
be constantly restrained as to costume. Her
idea of the dress of a country lass was a gay
wash silk gown and a lace and ribbon apron.

The days ran by and the eventful night came at last. A back stairway used by the servants was given over to the actors. Mrs. Baylor is in her room putting on the yachting dress which is to be her costume; the dress in which *Alice's* husband had turned her adrift in an open boat upon the sea, as a punishment for loving another man. She has her long hair down and is carefully dipping the ends of the strands into toilet water to give it the look of just emerging from the briny deep, when there is a knock at her door. She thinks it is her husband and calls out "*Entrez*," but the knock is repeated. She goes to the door and throws it open, and sees Reginald Courtney standing there in his light keeper's costume.

The corduroy, the flannel shirt open at the neck, the sou' wester hat, all suit his manly figure and rugged face. Mary forgets her frillery of dressing sack and her hair on her shoulders, and looks at him admiringly.

"Oh, I beg your pardon," he says in confusion. "I thought—this was your parlor door. How could I have made such a mistake?"

"It's of no consequence. You'll have to come in here any way to be made up. Dick and Dolly are playing on the lounge. Come along in." And in he goes.

All over the dressing table are strewn bottles of cosmetic and sticks of grease paint in confusion. Everything is in disorder, but it is a perfumery, pretty disarray. Baylor half rises from his romp with the baby to greet Reg as he sits down to be manipulated, and then returns to the frolic with the child.

"Turn your face away from the glass," Mary says. "I want you to be astonished when you see yourself." And then she goes to work with the paints and sponges until Reg feels as though his face is being turned into a mask; but every touch of her finger tips sends a little shiver over him. They are very light and quite by chance touches she makes the material lay itself on, but her face is close to his. He can see the fine texture of her rosy skin, and the way her lashes curl back.

Baylor gets up, and taking Dolly on his arm, goes into the parlor.

" Wait one minute.   I want to see if Dick
is going out," and she runs after him.

There are dozens of trifling little trinkets
lying about on the table.   Reg thinks he
must have something of hers, something that
belongs to her.   There is a little scarlet sea
bean locket, the mounting gilt, a trifle worth
fifty cents, perhaps upon some long past day
when it was a fad to own such a thing.   Before
she comes back, he has stuck it in his pocket.
He feels like a thief one instant, and like a
knight wearing a lady's token the next, and
he glories in his sensations.   Real sensations
are so new to Reg.

He is allowed to look at himself, bedight
with the paint which the footlights will soften,
better looking than he ever was in his life.
Mary looks over his shoulder, delighted with
her handiwork.   The door has been left open
in the corridor only a few inches, but those
inches give full upon the two figures standing
before the mirror.   Some one comes along the
corridor, but neither hears.

" See here," Mary cries.   " You've got your

hair wrong." She seizes a brush and sets it right just as Edyth passes—half stops—and then blind with disgust and rage and mortification at what she sees, goes flying on into her own room to throw herself on the bed and choke her sobs in the pillow.

When Mrs. Courtney comes in a few minutes later to say in a resigned tone that she supposes as Reg is to take part in the play, there is nothing for them to do but to go down and see it, unless they want to set every tongue wagging, and she thinks Edyth had better wear her pink striped silk with the dark red velvet sleeves, she finds her future daughter in law in bed with her head tied up in a wet towel and barely voice enough to say that she has a frightful headache.

"It's all on account of the sun on the water. I *knew* it!" Mrs. Courtney says. "We certainly shall leave here *tomorrow*." And then she goes bustling back with various doses, all of which Edyth meekly swallows, only too glad to be let alone at any price. She begs Mrs. Courtney not to miss the play, and after an hour's dressing she is finally off down stairs, hot and creaking in her tight silk harness, her husband meekly following in her wake.

Edyth can hear the band, can hear the gay parties trooping down stairs, and then can hear the clapping as the curtain goes up. There is dead silence then for what seems to her hours. She wonders if it is a failure, and some way that seems to lighten the awful burden just a trifle, and then—there is applause that fairly rocks the house again and again. They are bowing their thanks down there, Mary radiant, because the gift that is in her has not grown dull with disuse. Reg, with her hand in his, and that guilty little red locket in his pocket, is not conscious enough of his state to know that the realization of his love will never come, and is happy. Up stairs Edyth turns her face to the wall with fresh, smarting tears.

X.

MARY had looked forward so long to this home coming at Ellenbro'. She had pictured in her mind the big, old fashioned Southern house, with its wide hallway and long verandas, and sunny slopes of garden. She had seen places, not grand places, but sweet, old fashioned homes here and there in her wandering about, and she had always dreamed of some time living in one. But Castle Hill is not the home of Mary's dreams. It is an old house, but instead of standing like a stately queen on a hill top, overlooking her glad domain, the early Baylor who conceived this mansion built it under the hill instead of on top, with an idea of sheltering the inmates. Its brick foundation has kept it damp, and the old vines which cling about its walls, and send strong shoots into the windows, give it a vault-like feeling.

The little station in Ellenbro' had not been
the pretty country stopping place she had expected, but a big, dirty "depot," crowded with
curious loafers. There was no one to meet
them, and the only vehicle which could take
them to their own roof tree was an old coupé,
dingy and hot, which hung about the station
in rain or shine, its horse drooping and its
driver asleep inside.

But none of these things daunted Mary's
happy spirits. She was going home! The
old home of Richard, the home that was to be
Dolly's. As they drive in at the gateway she
cannot believe that this can be the home she
has dreamed of. It has been in her mind's
eye so long as something so different. As they
rattled up the driveway, bordered on each side
by ragged syringa bushes and with gloomy old
Norway firs bordering the lane, she could not
believe at first that this was the place.

"Well, my dear," Baylor said, leaning out,
and looking at the old house. It had bored
him tremendously in the old days; bored him
so much that he had gone away and left it all

—all the darkness and closeness and conventional narrowness; shaken the dust from his feet; but now coming back it held for him something of the glamour of his boyhood. The world that he had dreamed of then had not turned out such a great thing after all, and now he was coming back with wife and child, it seemed as pleasant a place as any.

"I've no doubt it will be charming." Mary had thought of herself as clasping her hands and exclaiming with delight when she saw the house, but that, like so many anticipations, had faded before the reality. They had gone into the narrow, long, lofty rooms and had interviewed the two old servants who had stayed as caretakers. They were tired out. A chill little wind had come up from somewhere and the rooms had an odor of mildew.

Mr. Baylor put his hands in his trousers' pockets and walked about the room, looking at everything. It was all so familiar and yet so strange. It had been another person, a fresh, inexperienced boy who had taken this into his young memory, a memory that had

jostled the picture of these old rooms with
strange company since then.

"What is there for dinner?" he asked the
tall negro woman who had let them in.

"Ain't you done had no dinner? I was
'lowin' to give you a mess o' fried chicken fer
supper."

"That's all right. Call it what you've a
mind to," Baylor said good naturedly. "Only
hurry it up. I'm hungry."

"Build a fire in here, at once," Mary said.
"Dolly will catch her death of cold," she
added as she saw the blank astonishment on
the woman's face at the idea of wanting a fire
in the middle of summer. "It smells musty,
too—ugh!"

She went to the windows and threw them
up.

"Finical Yankee!" Cynthia muttered as she
went out. "Throwin' up the windows an'
wantin' a fire laid right here in August.
Never shook hands with a body, nor said
nothin'!"

Mary's heart was sick with disappointment.

Presently Cynthia's husband, Bob, came in with a basket of wood and laid a large fire, which was soon roaring up the chimney until the room was unbearable.

"They are not accustomed to anything but winter fires down here," Baylor said. The wind came tearing down the wide chimney and swept smoke and ashes out into the room in a choking cloud.

Mary took Dolly by the hand and went up stairs to investigate. The house was an old one, without any of the modern improvements. It had been hastily got ready by the two negroes who had served its former owner, but there had been no careful hand to see that it was made habitable. Miss Baylor had not felt that it came within her duties when Richard had not written to her of his coming.

At the supper table, where the tall, cross looking woman waited, Baylor tried to eat the chicken and put it back on the plate.

"When was this fowl killed?" he asked with suspicious calmness.

"This afternoon, sir."

"Just as I thought. Understand, will you, that no fowl is to come to this table that has not been hung up at least three days."

The woman had been housekeeper for years and had been absolute ruler.

"You didn't send word——" she began, but there was a look in Baylor's face which silenced her.

Dolly, tired, began to cry, deepening the line in her father's forehead. Mary quietly arose and took her up stairs.

"I wants to do *home!*" the baby sobbed, and as Mary put her to bed there were tears in her own eyes as she echoed the wish.

XI.

IN Ellenbro' everybody knows everybody else. In the summer evenings young girls in pretty, light dresses, whose outline holds some suggestion of the mode prevailing in the centers of civilization, but whose detail is painfully lacking, walk from lawn to lawn and talk of the two new topics of interest. Edyth Smith is engaged to Reginald Courtney, and the Richard Baylors have come to the old Baylor place.

"They say" (how many times "they say" does drop from the lips! It makes one think of the endless sequences that may be made out of a cribbage hand, by different combinations of the same cards) "that Mrs. Baylor is awfully pretty, and——" And then eyebrows are lifted. "Cynthia"—everybody knows Cynthia—"says that you could tell that she wasn't 'quality' by her airs." And then

the further tale of Cynthia was told; how
Miss Baylor had come to call and found Reginald Courtney there helping Mrs. Baylor
unpack her dresses. There was a little grain
of pleasure to these young girls—sweet, gentle,
young girls who were not engaged—in the
picture of Edyth Smith's lover being fastened
at Mrs. Baylor's chariot wheels. They couldn't
imagine what any man could see in Edyth
Smith, except, of course, her money. His
mother had made the match, no doubt; everybody had always known that she would do it
if she could. Edyth was a sweet girl, of
course, and a good girl, but she certainly was
stupid.

As for Mrs. Baylor, everybody was anxious
and waiting to see her. Nobody felt like going
to call, just at first. They would all wait and
see what would happen. Ladies looked at
each other a little significantly, and said they
would wait until Mrs. Baylor had finished her
unpacking.

None of this unpacking episode comes to
Edyth's ears just now. Mrs. Courtney has

heard it, but she is beginning to have a rather uneasy feeling about this engagement. She thinks it would not be well to harrow Edyth's feelings. Young men will be young men, and when Reg is safely married he will be like all the rest. The thing to do now is to announce the engagement far and wide, to bring in all the kin to congratulate, to tie Reg by a thousand ties of obligation, and to marry him and Edyth at the earliest possible moment. It behooves her in the mean time to keep Mrs. Baylor from entering any place where it would be likely that Reg would meet her. With the usual short vision that belongs to womankind, she does not see that by this means she gives him more opportunity to see Mrs. Baylor in her own home.

Before any real hostility has time to show itself, Ellenbro' is the center of a small excitement. Ellenbro' is the county seat, and this is the year of a presidential election. The prospective governor of the State is a relative of many of the Ellenbro' people, a distant cousin to the Courtneys. He is coming to speak, and with him are to be a number of politicians from the Eastern cities—among them a man of "magnetism," who has barely escaped the great nomination himself. The town is full—full with everybody, from the countryman in his big wagon, filled with straw, bed quilts, and children, to the "cousins" from the great places up the river. Everybody has come to hear the speeches, with the Southern love for oratory, and the town is lively and gay.

It is at this time that some enterprising citizeness sees a grand opportunity of "booming" the hospital. Now there never are in Ellenbro' any sick people who have not relatives and friends enough to take care of them, and carry them food which the family and servants eat, and stand on the outside of the door and ask in penetrating whispers "how they are today." But Ellenbro' is beginning to look about and notice the tricks and manners of other towns, and a hospital seems to be a fashionable adornment for a place of its size. Edyth Smith has given three hundred dollars toward it, and is an authority to consult. She

gives her voice in favor of a garden party to be
held on the day of the speeches. People
would come there for supper—dinner is served
at half past one in Ellenbro'—and then again
at night for ice cream.

The lawn of one of the prominent citizens,
a first cousin of the governor elect, was chosen
for its size and central location. Tables and
booths were put up all over it, and pretty girls
in capes and aprons were set behind them.
Edyth took charge of a candy table. It had
been her own choice, although half a dozen
prettier girls had wondered at her audacity in
getting in among those ribbons and boxes of
many colors. They had said so to each other,
but it had struck none of them to mention it
to Edyth herself.

There are very few people there for supper;
only business men whose wives are interested
in the hospital, and who know that there is
no prospect of food at home ; and the rector
of the parish, and a few old ladies. The
young girls behind the tables stand nervously
—waiting. They have all taken Edyth's

hand and congratulated her in set terms upon her engagement. There has been none of the girl talk which would have flowed apace had one of themselves become engaged. Edyth's money, and her constant overlooking by Mrs. Courtney, have in a measure set her apart from the other girls. There is a lack which she feels, but she knows no way to overcome it.

But later, after the speeches are over in the evening, the place begins to fill up. It looks very bright with the Japanese lanterns among the trees, and people in gay gowns walking about and sitting at little tables on the green lawn. The moon that had lightened up everything at Atlantic City is an old moon now, waxing thin, and taking its time about coming up, but the headlights of locomotives and many candles and lamps have taken its place, though they leave plenty of dark, sequestered nooks.

Mrs. Courtney had gone to supper, and then to hear the speeches, expecting to find Reginald and bring him with her. She comes back a little put out, with only the general—

bland and good natured, with his perpetual air of thinking about something else, principally his ancestors—as her companion. Edyth stands half proud and half ready to cry, her disappointment is so keen. Poor girl! This is no sort of an engagement at all, when she has to stand and wonder what her sweetheart is going to do next. She knows enough about the conventional engaged girl to know that she is usually for that time, if never again in her life, the center of her little world, the queen from whose throne commands may flow.

Edyth is becoming more and more uncomfortable, and Mrs. Courtney is growing decidedly angry. The band has come up from the big wooden "wigwam" where the speeches have been made, escorting the carriages which hold the heroes of the hour. "See the Conquering Hero Comes" has been exhausted long ago, and the strains of "After the Ball"—considered modish in Ellenbro'—are wafted over the lawn. Edyth leaves her booth at Mrs. Courtney's command and begins a slow promenade about the paths, on General Courtney's other arm. They are just turning the corner where the table has been spread for the refreshment of the distinguished guests, when—there before them, laughing and talking, having the very best imaginable time—caring not in the least for the Courtneys, Ellenbro', or its world, is Mrs. Richard Baylor.

On one side of her is a young man, and on the other an old one, both equally solicitous, and equally ready to look when she looks and see as she sees. One is the cabinet officer of the day, and the other is Reginald Courtney.

There is a whole artillery of anger going off in Edyth's heart. She feels the blood fairly tearing through her veins, but she says never a word. She has a feeling toward Mrs. Baylor that is almost pitiful. She hates her, and she dreads her, and she does not think she is a good woman, but she feels ready enough to let her alone, if only she may be left to enjoy her little world. "With so many," Edyth thinks, "she might let Reg alone." To chide Reg, to send him away, is beyond her power.

"Why!" the general begins, but he gets no

farther than his exclamation. There is a pressure upon his arm which seems to draw his eyes. There has been telegraphed to his inner consciousness the information that he is not to look in Mrs. Baylor's direction. All three of them stalk solemnly by.

They are past before Reg realizes who it is; and then he starts—he half starts, or he half begins to start—after them. But they have seemed so utterly unconscious of any one's presence that his thick masculine sense believes they did not see him. Mrs. Baylor is just telling such a clever story—or is it just one of her crisp sentences? He hardly knows. He only knows that she is looking up at the distinguished visitor in such a way that he cannot bear to leave him to take it in all alone. His people have gone on. He will join them presently, and he lingers, listening and looking.

It never occurs to the distinguished visitor that he is not talking to the most popular woman on the ground, and it is not occurring to Reg that he is not by any means assisting Mrs. Baylor's popularity. The distinguished visitor knows a pretty woman when he sees one. He has heard that this one is a Baylor, and has immediately asked for an introduction to her. Reg has been standing there, and as he knows her, and no one else does, it has been for him to offer to present the guest. Ten minutes later, Mary is walking about the lawn on the arm of the guest of the city, with all Ellenbro' looking on.

XII.

MR. BAYLOR had stood looking about him after the distinguished visitor had been introduced to his wife and had shaken his own hand with the firm and cordial clasp of the politician. The whole thing rather bored him. He had come because he had within him the determination to show people that his wife had no shrinking in regard to her new position; that he was proud of her and meant to sustain the place to which she was entitled.

Then, too, the sight of Ellenbro' society was a comedy to him. He thought several times, as he had often thought in the theaters he frequented, that it was a comedy whose coloring and setting could be changed to advantage. Baylor had ideas of playwriting himself. It was in the vague and desultory studies that he was making for that play which never was and never would be written, that he first met Mary.

"The material is here, I suppose. Now there is a figure——" Baylor put on his eyeglasses and looked again. Then he took them off, and stood fumbling with them while his wife talked, with a queer, abstracted smile on his impassive face. Then he put them up and went slowly across the lawn.

Standing by a tree and talking to two or three old ladies, with a look of interest upon her blonde face, was a woman past her first youth, but with a certain daintiness that would always be charming. She was very simply gowned, in the usual Ellenbro' cut of garments, but while there was none of that elusive quality called style, of which Mary Baylor owned such an abundance, there was a sweetness of demeanor that seemed to make up for any lack of purely material things. Her hair was too light to show any hint of gray, and there was almost a virginal look in her eyes. Richard Baylor stopped before her. She gave a little start, the color flashing up in her smooth cheeks, and impulsively her hand went out to meet his.

"How do you do"—there was the most
trifling pause—"Mr. Baylor? It is a pleasure
to see an old friend after all these years." The
voice was as silky as the hair.

The smile was still on Baylor's face. "It
seems like yesterday," he said. The heads of
the two old ladies were almost together, and
their black gloved fingers touched each other
under the lace of their capes. They remembered
when Dick Baylor and Nannie Vance were
boy and girl sweethearts. It only seemed like
yesterday; and here was she, a widow these
half dozen years, and Dick Baylor just home
with his young wife.

It was of this young wife that Mrs. Rogers
spoke at once. She was not the woman to
ignore any of the minor conventionalities. "I
hope you will introduce me to Mrs. Baylor.
I see she is making quite an impression upon
our great man. She is very pretty. I believe"—she looked up and laughed with an
infantile glance and a glimpse of little, white
teeth—"you always liked pretty women."

"Yes," Baylor said, still with that smile.

"And clever? You always liked clever women, too."

He had never given much thought to the question whether Mary was clever or not. He never cared. In his heart he rather thought she was, but in his mind he rather thought she wasn't. Clever—yes, for her world, but hardly for this one.

But Mrs. Rogers was clever. One was never allowed to forget that fact. She had been clever in her soft, purring way when she had said good by to Dick Baylor, the rather erratic boy, and married Mr. Rogers, who owned the large factory across the river. Dick had carried off his disappointment—if he felt any—so easily that in Ellenbro', where women make public opinion, and where they are loath to let another woman have one sweetheart of her own, much less two, he was never looked upon as a jilted man. It would have made little difference to him, as the verdict of Ellenbro' was of small consequence one way or another.

Now, when he saw Mrs. Rogers looking at him with Nannie Vance's old manner, there was no wounded vanity to stand in the way of his greeting. He was honestly glad to look over this almost unchanged page out of his old life. To be sure, he had forgotten it—almost entirely. Nannie Vance had been no factor in his home coming, but he accepted, in his usual lazy fashion, the goods that the gods sent.

"I never liked a stupid woman, surely. I never knew many." He looked about the grounds. Many of the faces were those he had seen from infancy, and there was little change to his eyes. There was some dust in them, perhaps, from years and indifference, and he hardly saw things as clearly as he once had seen them. Age is after all a mere matter of comparison.

"No, you never knew Ellenbro' very well," Mrs. Rogers said sedately. "You never would. And have you come back to the old place to live?"

It was all the quietest of talk.

Mary, meanwhile, walked about the lawn with Reginald and the guest. The guest of the hour walking with as pretty and charming a woman as Mrs. Baylor, naturally formed a sort of nucleus. Gentlemen came up to speak to the honorable, and stayed to talk to the newcomer. It was all so gay and pleasant. She looked around at the others who walked and sat about, and she saw the glances that came her way. She also saw that she wore the only gown there whose outline was modish. In Mary there were, and always would be, the instincts of the actress. An audience keyed her up. She played to it as unconsciously as a flower opens to the sunlight. She felt the glances and the comments that were all about her, and her face took on its merriest lines and her voice its gayest notes.

It has not escaped her keen vision that Mrs. Courtney and Edyth have gone by with unseeing eyes. There has been a little color that has grown warm in her cheeks as she sees it. She wants to turn to Reg and tell him to go back to his own people; and then she blames herself for uncharitableness. How can the boy help that his people are illbred and stiff? She knows that it must mortify him, and

she gives him an extra kind look to make up
for it.

There is nothing about Mary to indicate her
theatrical origin.   Her thin, crisp gown with
its little bows and rosettes of ribbon, has no
theatrical cut, with all its look of vogue.   Her
dark, smooth hair has no eccentric quirks of
dressing, and her smooth, almost childlike skin
is innocent of any aids to freshness.   Ellenbro'
takes refuge in remembering Mrs. Courtney's
report from Atlantic City and the story of
Miss Baylor's morning call.   And then—well,
there must be a *something* that men recognize.

"How did he know that she was that sort
of person?" one matron asks another, indicat-
ing Mary and the distinguished visitor.   "He
wanted to be introduced to her at once.   He
recognized the *difference.*"

"He probably knew her in New York," the
other said cynically.   "And, any way, he has
seen enough of the world to classify."

In one of her turns Mary catches a glimpse
of the face she is always looking for.   She
isn't a jealous woman.   She never has been a

jealous woman. She has always seen her husband turn wearily away from women's society. She has seen him put on his stillest face of weariness when sometimes one came their way, and she has taken no thought that her peace of mind depended in a great measure upon this.

There is a generous, lavish heart in Mary, but that very lavishness is an outcome of the rapid pulse that makes her claim her own. It had been long since she had seen on Richard Baylor's face just that look of interest. In an instant everything is forgotten except the little gnawing pain that springs out and startles her. With a natural impulse she stats toward her husband, and then, for the first time since she has been his wife, she draws back.

Cousin James MacIntyre had spoken kindly to Edyth, with his eyes everywhere and his palm ready to clasp every other, and then had forgotten all about her.

"I think," Edyth suggested, "that we had better go home."

"No," Mrs. Courtney said firmly. "We are not going home yet." There was a firm set about her mouth. She had in view the social demolition of this troublesome young woman. "Excessively bad taste to come and force herself where she was not invited," she added.

"But nobody was invited, were they, my dear?" It was seldom the general went beyond boundaries well known to him.

"That is exactly the bad taste. They should have waited to make their appearance at something to which invitations were issued."

"And to which they would not have been asked."

"*Certainly* not."

The general hadn't much sense of humor, or he would never, even in callowest youth, have married Mrs. Courtney; but there is a little line of smile under his mustache—a line that fades out in loneliness, having no companion gleam.

The great guest is reminded that there is a supper to be eaten and that people are waiting for him, and he goes off reluctantly, hoping to

see Mrs. Baylor very soon again. Reg and
Mary are left alone, she a trifle out of time.

"It is a lovely night," Reg says, with start-
ling originality.

"No. Is it? I hadn't thought so. I believe it is going to rain. It is surely time to
go home."

Everything has grown stale and stupid in
these last minutes. Mary looks about again,
and sees nothing of her husband. There are
so many dark little nooks about the grounds.
She has not sufficient knowledge of the real
social world to know that her husband and
Mrs. Rogers would be as little likely to seek one
of those secluded spots, as to dance a fandango
on the green.

They walk on and on. Reginald feels the
chill that has come into the atmosphere, and
instead of finding Mrs. Baylor stupid, as he
would be likely to find any other woman
under the circumstances, he chides himself for
his inability to entertain her. The band plays
gay music, and she stops and listens, a soft
little look in her face. There is one old tune,

the " My Queen " waltz, that has seemed to pulse and throb through so much of her life. The orchestra outside was playing it the night she met Richard, and the band is playing it now. She stops Reg where they can hear it, perfectly oblivious of the fact that around and about her is a critical throng, and that the Courtneys are looking her over. Reg has grown reckless. He doesn't care the very least in the world. With all the doggedness that is in him he has enrolled himself in the ranks of Mrs. Baylor's friends, and he means to stand by her. It looks such a manly and sweet and simple thing to do. The duty that he owes to Edyth is entirely lost sight of.

It is a curious phenomenon in the brain of man, that when he is in love—(oh, Reg, you have not named it, but the rest of us have!)— he has a single vision. He can see nothing whatever that does not concern the object of his affections. She is the one center toward which all his actions radiate. It seems to him right and just that he should take up Mrs. Baylor's cause and fight it out to the end.

After all, instinct is the very strongest force that is in us. Every action that is of consequence is bred by it. We may civilize our emotions, but they arise up and break their bonds and laugh at us, in any crisis. Nature is the great guide who whips us all into line, and who scorns the puny laws of men.

"But," Mrs. Rogers is saying over on the other side, where she and Baylor still stand idly talking, "there is your wife. I want to meet her." She says it with an air of condescension which rather amuses Baylor than otherwise.

"Certainly, Mrs. Baylor will be delighted;" and he offers his arm.

They are all drifting down in front of Mrs. Courtney, where she sits in august majesty and a stiff and provincial black silk, Edyth and the general keeping her company. It is at this especially and particularly inopportune moment that Cousin James MacIntyre leaves his supper and has a flash of memory. He has heard of Reg's engagement, and he has not congratulated him. Of course this pretty woman must be the betrothed. With the utmost desire to make himself agreeable he walks over to Reg and Mrs. Baylor, declines to be introduced to his "almost cousin," and hilariously congratulates Reg upon his approaching marriage with Mary Baylor. And Edyth sits and hears it all!

The offense is by no means palliated by the fact that Mrs. Rogers and Richard Baylor also hear it, and seem to consider it most amusing. Mary's face is her own sweet one again at the approach of her husband, and while her pretty cheeks flush a little, she too enjoys the joke. Reginald's emotion goes deeper than any one dreams. Until now his feeling for Mrs. Baylor has been vague. Suddenly the wild thought of the "might have been" flashes through his mind, leaving him pale, with a flutter about his heart.

Mrs. Rogers stopped and said her pleasant words to the wife of her old sweetheart, and invited her to drive home in her carriage. Reg put Mrs. Baylor in and then went back to his legitimate affections.

As Mary and her husband let themselves in at their own door, so different from the little entrance to their flat in New York, and groped their way about through the shadows which the kerosene lamp threw into the gloomy corners of the dark hall, she suddenly stopped and put her hand upon the lapel of his coat. He turned about, and she looked so eager, so pretty, so anxious, out of all those black shadows, that he promptly kissed her.

"Dick," she said, "who is Mrs. Rogers?"

"Mrs. Rogers? Oh, she was a girl I used to know, long ago. Her name was Nannie Vance. She married a man old enough to be her father, and he died a few years ago."

"She is in love with you."

"Polly, my dear, if I listened to you, I should be the most conceited man on this earth."

"You are—almost," Polly said, laughing.

Baylor picked up a package which was lying on the spindled legged card table in the hall. "Here is our mail. One from Poncet, and —hello! A letter for you that looks as though some of your charity people had written it."

XIII.

THERE was little sleep for Edyth that
night. She turned her pillow again and
again. She felt years older than she had felt
a month ago. She almost wished—with tears
falling down her cheeks and dropping, as is
the way with easily shed tears, in round
splashes upon the white pillow case—that she
had never become engaged to Reg. She made
up her mind that she would break with him
at once, and let him go and flirt with his horrid
married woman.

And then she realized that that wouldn't
mend the business at all. Reginald, by asking her to marry him, had put into form a
something that she could not analyze. It was
the sense of possession. She felt that all her
pride, all the woman in her, grew up to prevent this other woman from taking from her
what was hers. She had hardly spoken to Reg

all the way home, and had gone up to her
room before he said good night, slipping away
from formalities in the way that is so easy in
a great, many windowed house.

What had promised to be her triumph had
been her humiliation, but she was gaining in
pride. The idea that Reg could ask her to
marry him when he did not love her, she could
not understand. He must love her. A man
always, in her world, asked a woman to marry
him because he cared more for her than for
anything else on earth. The idea of Reg
thinking of her money never had the slightest
entrance into her mind. Her money had done
too little for her, that she could see, for her
to realize its value in the eyes of other people.

Edyth was young and healthy. Before she
had become so miserable she had eaten a
hearty supper, so she finally went to sleep; but
in the morning she awoke with the first gray-
ness of the dawn with that sense of heaviness,
of disaster, of unnamed sorrow, which follows
a waking when sleep has come to a heavy
heart.

The heavy boughs of the maples were dew laden against her casement, and all the air was full of the busy stir of birds. She could not lie still, and she could not think of getting up to face them all at breakfast. She opened the casement and looked out. The river lay clear and cool in the distance, and along its rather rugged banks, along the bluff above, ran a road fringed by alders, goldenrod, and iron-weed. She could see the river mists hanging ragged on the branches.

There came around the corner of the house the shrill whistle of Yellow Bob on his way to the stables. Edyth put her head out of the window.

"Bob!" she cried.

"Yessum!"

"Saddle Gladys." (Poor Edyth! Even in naming her pretty brown mare she had had no imagination, but had called it by the name she would have given a baby.) "I am going to ride."

"Fo'h sun up?"

"Now."

"All right'm."

There was a strangeness in the world; it was as though it were new. Edyth had never done such a thing as this before. The mare seemed to feel her mood and adapt herself to it. They went springing over the turf of the field that led through to the river road, and then the horse's feet were brisk on the road's hard whiteness.

Edyth hardly knew how long she had ridden. She did not come back to the river road, but turned off into another, which ran through a little glen. The sun had grown hot, and she needed food. It looked very cool and inviting down in there, and she rode her horse over the almost spongy turf that led down the hillside into the glen. She dismounted, careful of her dress and her gloves, and, taking off her hat, sat down by the side of a fern shaded little spring.

There was a stillness all about her and a shadow. The spring was wide again on the other side of the bunch of willows, and there was another hollow. Edyth had not been here

since the year before, and she was wondering
how it looked on the other side. There used
to be some raspberry canes over in there. She
wondered if there was any late fruit on them,
and half started up to see, but was arrested by
a voice—a voice whose every tone she had
grown to dread and hate—Mary Baylor's.

Then she remembered that she was on the
Baylor place. Of course Mary's companion
was Reg. Edyth felt that it must be so. She
sat still as though she had not the volition to
move. She did not want to hear what they
were saying, but she had not the courage to
get up and let them see her there. And so she
sat still.

"Please go away," Mrs. Baylor's voice was
saying plaintively. There were almost tears
in it. "Please, oh *please*, go away! I can do
nothing more for you, and if Mr. Baylor were
to know about you——"

"I don't know what he could say to me,
that hasn't been said already," said a bitter
voice that was a man's, but yet not Reg's. "I
have had the whole catalogue of vituperation

flung at me from one quarter or another, and——" there was a throaty laugh which sounded as though the vocal chords had been through very rough usage—"I think I can claim the credit of having deserved it all. But you, Polly, you never were like that."

"Can't you understand," Edyth hears her say, "that everything is different now? I am married. I have a little girl. I do not want my husband—my child——"

"To know, eh? Well, it isn't exactly kind. But I am a very sick man. You are the only friend I have in the world. I wanted to come down here and see it all before I died."

"Don't! Oh, *don't!*"

A touch of red came into Edyth's cheeks. "Oh, mine enemy!" her heart seemed to say, "so you have a secret to hide!"

Edyth was frightened at the intensity of her own feeling. She had never expected to be a listener. Yesterday she would have scorned doing anything so dishonorable, but today— she opened wide her ears.

"Does it bother you so much, Polly?"

There was almost gentleness in the voice.
"Well, I will go away again. I am glad to
have seen you, though. I rather thought I
might see you now and then—and I should
like to see your baby. I am—" he laughed
again—"absolutely disreputable, I know, but
nobody could hurt you or yours, Polly."

"Poncet is coming down. I have a letter
from him. He would know you. It would be
a secret between us. You must—oh, won't
you?—go away."

"Yes, if I—can."

"Please, oh please, *promise* me!"

Gladys made a noise with her foot. Edyth
could fairly hear the silence that followed;
and then there was the sound of people moving
away.

XIV.

EDYTH hardly knew how long she sat there; long enough to have created dozens of conversations in which she could tell Reg all that she had overheard. She did not think of going home and telling it to her aunt. The girl had gone beyond that stage, and had come to the realization of her own independent womanhood.

As she rode up through the shadow of the glen, she passed a man who she felt sure must be the one that had been speaking to Mrs. Baylor. He looked like a gentleman whose manners and morals had grown seedy with his clothes. There was a half attempt at respectability, whose gloss was taken off by a glance at the dissipated face, worn with enough life to have killed half a dozen men. There was a something about the figure that looked foreign or theatrical. Theatrical, Edyth called it, because the foreign flavor was outside her knowledge or comprehension. She looked at him with fear and disgust, and yet with a sort of pleasure, too. Truly she need never fear Mrs. Baylor again, after she had told her story to Reg.

It was afternoon when she arrived at home and found General and Mrs. Courtney out on the veranda looking for her, and Reginald on horseback about to go in search of her.

"There she is now," her aunt said, with a worried look. "Where *have* you been?"

"For a little ride. I went farther than I intended, and came home by the glen road."

Mrs. Courtney suddenly turned to her husband, as though he were responsible. "Wasn't it on the glen road that Bob saw that queer looking man yesterday? My dear Edyth, you must not go out unless Reginald is with you. He has been so anxious that he was about to start after you."

"Yes, I was going to start after you," Reg said, turning himself in his saddle and dismounting to lift Edyth to the ground, "but I did you and the mare the compliment of thinking you could take care of yourselves. But if you had told me, and waited for a breakfast, I should have been delighted to go with you."

In the new knowledge of Mrs. Baylor which Edyth possessed, and in her knowledge of Reg's opinions upon some subjects, she had come to consider him as her own again. The feeling had been strengthened by the sight of him, big and stalwart, a modern knight in corduroy, setting out to rescue his lady love from unknown terrors. It was a little dampening to know that he had been ordered out and was going with a laugh.

" There is a luncheon inside for you, and I am coming in to help you eat it," Reg said. " I was started off with a snatched crust."

"Come along," Edyth cried gaily. She looked almost pretty, she was so happy and elated—innocent, good little Edyth !—over the downfall of this other woman. Reg had probably known what sort of person she was all along, and while it was not very respectful in him to parade about with her before his mother and his sweetheart, still, that ought to be forgiven.

"I'll be there. Get your hat off."

It was a substantial luncheon that the maid put on the table when she knew that Miss Edyth was coming in hungry. Substantial meals were served at the Courtneys' every day, as was consistent with all the other family appointments. Edyth sat down to it with a keen relish. She had laid out her line of tactics. She was going to tell Reg the story, as she would tell him a story about any one else. She would ignore the fact of his more than casual acquaintance with Mrs. Baylor.

Reg was in his best humor. He had kept his horse at the door, and he was going to ride over to the Baylor estate this very afternoon. From former experiences he knew that Mrs. Baylor at her most gracious was Mrs. Baylor at home. There were a few arbors and quaint, rickety old summerhouses about Castle Hill. Mary and Dolly were a pair of merry companions with whom to while away the hours.

Sometimes Baylor came out under the trees and smoked a cigar. It was seldom enough that Reg could be induced to smoke a cigar in the society of his divinity. To Dick Baylor, Reg is the veriest boy, a callow stripling. He looks at him sometimes, and wonders in an idle fashion what Polly finds in his society to amuse her, and presently comes to the conclusion that she sets him at errands. "And a good thing, too," he thinks. "I'm past errand running myself."

Such an insight into enjoyment of simple living as Reg gets from this household is a revelation to him. He has never known people to whom the light of day, the sun overhead, the simple every day pleasures, were of paramount importance. People in Ellenbro'—the people he had known all of his life—were always living for the vision of their neighbors. Every act was not first of all for the pleasure of it, but that it might make some sort of an impression upon the neighborhood. When Mary was at home she enjoyed up to the edge every minute of the glad day. She was a gay, jolly, merry hearted girl, whose heart held not one grain of malice toward any soul on earth. Sometimes her sense of humor made her see the fun in people.

"There are people," she said one day to Reg, "who are so funny that I cannot see why they are not perpetually entertained by their own society."

But whatever she said there was never in anything the least sting of ill nature.

There floated in his mind's eye a vision of her, in her simple white gown and gay hat, idling away the time about the hillside of her lawn, amusing Dolly, waiting for him to come. He knew that she would lift Dolly up, and be unaffectedly glad to see him, and that she would tell him so. There were smiles at the corners of his mouth as he thought of it. It was a little early to go. He looked at the tall, solemn old clock in the dining room, and thought that he could very profitably kill half an hour talking to Edyth, and eating the remainder of his luncheon.

Edyth had come down stairs after Reg had

begun to knock his heels on the floor and
frown a little impatiently. Poor Edyth had
not the knowledge of dress any more than she
had the knowledge of any gift of the imagination. She had a fondness for wrappers. If
there is one thing more than another that re-
quires to be idealized it is a wrapper. There
must be an idealization both of wearer and
gown. With Edyth there was neither. A
wrapper, to her, was a plain, unpoetic wrapper,
made neatly, and strictly for business, of plain,
dotted cambric, well washed and starched. It
was clean and ugly, and the wearer was sun-
burned and plain. She had dabbed cologne
water, a scent which Reg hated, upon her hair,
and pushed it back from her heated brow.
She looked as practical as bread and butter
and roast beef. She came in oddly upon Reg's
vision of that other woman's frills and coquet-
tish bows, so innocently donned.

"Where did you go this morning?" he asks,
as he carefully puts the ingredients of a salad
dressing into a wooden spoon and stirs them
around. "Did you stop anywhere?"

"I got off for a little while by the spring in the glen."

"I wouldn't go that road alone, Edyth."

"It seems to be safe enough for some people. I saw one of your friends there this morning." This was exactly what she had intended not to say. She was to ignore that Mrs. Baylor was a friend.

"Who was that?"

There was nothing for it but to go on. "Mrs. Baylor."

"Was she riding?" Reg had no idea how much eagerness went into his voice. He had asked Mrs. Baylor if she rode over and over again, but she had always laughed and said she was afraid she would fall off.

"No," Edyth said icily. "She seemed to have walked. I only heard her. She was on one side of the spring, behind the trees, when I was on the other. She had evidently made an appointment there with a man—a man who looked like a dissipated tramp. She was begging him to go away and keep out of her husband's way; not to annoy her in her new life.

I presume it was some one of her early associates who knows more about her early life
than she cares to have known."

Edyth was not a virago, but her voice had
gone on and on, gaining in intensity as her
anger against this woman arose. She had not
looked at Reg's face. It was perfectly white.

"And you"—he could hardly speak. "And
you—stood and *listened*, and came away to
garble fragments of a private conversation not
intended for your ears! I have heard that
there was no honor in women—some women
—who call themselves *good*. Let me tell you
that I do not believe that there is one second
in Mrs. Baylor's life that she would hide from
the world. I know that she would never take
advantage of another woman behind her back!"
And the foolish, hot headed, hot hearted young
gallant walks out of the room, and comes very
near slamming the door.

XV.

IF one of the chairs had suddenly shot out an arm and struck him, Reg would not have been more astonished than he was by this new development of character in Edyth. There had been weakness and shyness and some obstinacy—the obstinacy of ignorance, embroidered with not much symmetry upon the native goodness of her character ; but this "downright meanness," as Reg called it angrily to himself, was something unpardonable.

He flung himself upon his horse, and naturally went straight toward Mrs. Baylor's, because he had learned from experience that he was always soothed by the sound of Mary's voice and the touch of little Dolly's baby arms. He found Mary walking feverishly about, a new color in her cheeks and an impatient tremble in her hands.

"I am so glad to see you," she said. Her heart was going in her bosom like a spinning ball, and she welcomed anything that took her out of herself. Perhaps an older man would have seen that there was something troubling her, that she was looking for a diversion—any diversion, and took the first one that came to hand. He would have felt the fever in the hot little hand as it touched his own; he would have seen the evidences of a disturbed mind, in the careful toilet that must have taken much longer than usual to make.

"I am very glad to be here," Reg said rather tamely. He was so honest, he had so few fine phrases in his vocabulary; he was so un-accustomed to needing them. "Where is Dolly?" He looked about for the merry little figure, that was always ready to climb upon his knee, and hunt for treasures in his pockets.

"Dolly?" with indifference. "She is happy in a new discovery. There is a brook that runs through the place. 'Willow Pond,' they call it, although why 'pond,' I'm sure I don't know."

"Oh, yes! I cut all my whistles there as a youngster. It's a famous place for catfish. Did you ever catch a catfish?"

"No, I never did, but I'd like to."

"Well——"

"Let's!"

"Get your hat." Reg had been ordering Edyth about ever since she was a very young child, and still owned that privilege, which was perhaps the reason he valued it so little. It may also have been the reason he felt such a sense of manly power in sending Mrs. Baylor after her hat. She came back in a moment with it on, looking ten times as pretty as she had without it.

"Who is with Dolly?" he asked, more for something to say than anything else, because he expected it to be her father, and Mary knew what picture of the father and child was in his mind. Her own face clouded over.

"A colored girl," she said shortly. They walked along in silence for a few minutes.

"Mr. Baylor went out this afternoon to make some calls," Mary said then.

"Did he?" Embarrassment was in Reg's voice. He was wondering where in the mischief Richard Baylor could be calling, and he was acutely conscious that Mary must know what he was thinking of.

"What a cad the man must be," he thought to himself, "to go to call upon people who have not been to see his wife."

"An old friend, whom he met at the garden party," Mary went on.

"Oh!"

They were walking along through the meadow. The sun was on the timothy and clover, bringing out all its sweetness. The second crop had not been cut, but was waiting to be "turned under" to enrich the soil. It was ragged and clumpy, but sweet, and the bees were blundering and honey gathering in the dull red blossoms.

"Do you like the country?" Reg remarked.

"I used to think I loved it," she said after a moment, "but perhaps it was only my idea of it. I used to look at the stage country, and think it was simply heaven. I think there are a great many things that we see the semblance of, and think we should be perfectly happy if we only had them in reality, which would disappoint us dreadfully if they really came our way."

Reg said nothing, but he looked down at her, and a sigh came in his throat. He only switched at the timothy tops and was silent. They were nearing the fringe of willows which defined the "pond," a narrow stream with deep holes here and there where it turned; holes where disobedient little boys loved to gather in the stolen delight of "goin' in swimmin'." They could hear Dolly's shrill little screams of delight, and in an instant see her dancing about upon her little bare pink toes, her flower of a white sunbonnet pushed back from her face. She was leaning over a tin pail.

"Can you catch any more?" she was inquiring excitedly. "I'm goin' to take this one home and pet it, and maybe it can be cooked for Dick's supper." When Dolly loved her father more dearly than usual she called him Dick.

"Not much of a supper's mess o' fish kin you ketch this here way," the negro girl said. She had a stout barrel hoop in her hand, to which had been fastened a sort of bag made of several thicknesses of mosquito netting. She was using it as a seine, dipping up now and then a minnow or a sunfish, or a little catfish.

Dolly ran to her mother when she saw her, wild with delight. "It makes me feel about five years old," Mary said. "I'd like to go wading in Willow Pond and catch fish myself."

"Why don't you?"

She laughed a little oddly and looked at him. "I don't know that it would be any different from wading about as we used to do at Trouville, in France. It seems a little different, though, to be doing—well, anything odd here in America."

"They say there are no people so odd and unconventional as Americans."

"Oh, yes! Americans in Europe. They are odd enough. But there isn't any place where an odd thing is as odd as it is in

America." She looked longingly at the seine and at the cool brook, at her shoes that only needed a pull at a ribbon to come off, and then back at Reg. Honestly in her heart she saw no possible reason why she shouldn't take off her shoes and stockings and wade in the water. Brook water and sea water, Atlantic City and Ellenbro', are much the same. But there was something in the boy's face that stopped her.

"Oh, no, it hardly does to forget one's years. Dolly will have no respect for her mother's age and wisdom if she sees me paddling about catching fish."

She sat down on the bank, looking away in another direction, and took her big hat off. Her dress was cut low around her pretty white neck, and she had gathered her soft dark hair up in a knot and run a white ribbon through it. There was a wistful expression in Mary's face, as it settled into quietness after the merriment that had swept over her at the thought of a possible "lark."

Reg was young; and there was a touch of

something upon his pulse which weighed heavier every hour. He was close to Mary, closer than he had been since the night of the theatricals, when he carried her in. The thought of her taking off her shoes and stockings to wade in the brook had struck his imagination as the fact of her really doing it would never have done. He thought of all sorts of things that he would like to say to her. He was astonished at his own audacity in thinking them; and yet he lingered delightedly over them. It is almost impossible to put two young people down together—wise old Poncet had thought it all out as he had seen them together—and not have the subject which was made for boys and girls come up between them.

It seemed to Reg that there was inspiration in the air.

"How pretty it is out here," Mary said, pulling at the grass beside her. "But then almost any place is pretty sometimes;" and she sighed.

"Any place is pretty, it seems to me, if you have the people you care for with you."

Do you ever think that?" she asked him wonderingly.

He reddened under her gaze. "Why shouldn't I think that? Haven't I an understanding?"

"Yes, but—you never have struck me as having been in love, even the little bit that men call being in love."

"What do you mean by being in love?" he asked her.

She opened her mouth two or three times, just parting her lips to speak. It was very sunny and quiet down there by the brook. They were sitting on the bank with their feet hanging over to the pebbles. Dolly was hilariously seining for minnows further up, the sun and shade dappling her white gown and plump little pink legs as they moved through the water. Mary pulled a blade of grass and drew it through her fingers as though it were new and strange.

"I don't believe in men's love at all. They are never constant except in books. People write books full of stuff—men who die for

people they love, but I notice "—there was a
cynical gleam in Mrs. Baylor's eye—"that
their taking off is usually complicated with
other diseases. Look down deep enough and
there is usually some other motive cropping
out. Sometimes, I know, they hardly know it
themselves. They think——" and then Mary
stopped. She did not truly believe that there
was any underlying " motive " in Dick's love
for her in those old days. There never had
been any doubt of it until the last day or two,
when she saw him with his own people, who
utterly refused to be her people.

"What do they think ? " Reg's voice was
not exactly within his own control.

" They think a woman will stand anything."

Reg hated Baylor because he was who he
was. This new joy that had come into his heart
was so innocent that it had not made him
ignoble, had not caused that disintegration
that seems to begin at every point in a character under the dissolving influence of an unlaw-
ful passion. He was not far enough gone to

be glad that Baylor was making her unhappy, seeing in this an opportunity for himself.

"It is a coward who would make a woman like you stand anything," he said with sudden vehemence.

She turned her face to his with every bit of color out of it. "What right have you to say that to me?" There is cool scorn—utter repudiation of everything, it seems to him—in her voice, and it heats instead of cools his blood. "What are you to me?"

"Nothing at all to you, I suppose," poor Reg says hotly, "but you know perfectly well that you are everything to me. You know that, from the very first instant I saw you, I have had no choice but to follow where you led. You know I wouldn't have it otherwise."

Oh, good and conventional woman, there is but one thing for you to do in a case like this. All the highly moral books have told you long, long ago what is expected of you, just as all the bad books have told you, with nicety of detail, what is done by those others in whom the prayerbook says there is "no health." But

Mary Baylor has been brought up in the natural school. She does not lift her skirts, arise, and move away, sorrow and scorn in her eyes, nor does she narrow her eyes and calculate, and think that her hour of revenge has come. She associates both of these attitudes with the stage, and she is playing neither the part of the ingenue nor that of the adventuress.

She turns around, and the color comes back into her face. A little curl starts up at each corner of her mouth, as she opens it to say, " Well, of all the young fools ! "

" I know I'm a fool," Reg says, "and I suppose you couldn't help making one of me. I suppose I made myself. You couldn't help being yourself, I suppose."

" My dear boy, your suppositions are mainly correct. I'm perfectly sure that I cannot help being myself, and I do not want to help it. But I deny having made a fool of you." She really looks at him in wonder. If Dolly had slapped her she would hardly have been more surprised. "Don't be silly. Why, I *like* you. You are just like my young brother, or like what he ought to be. I can—I thought I could—talk to you about anything. Why, you are a boy."

"I don't believe you have a heart," Reg dolefully replies.

"Oh, yes, I have," Mary says, rising; "and there is no room for another there. It has more to bear than a boy like you ever ought to know of. Go back to your sweetheart, that —nice girl." Mary is polite, but she is honest, and she has never seen anything in Edyth to bring out any complimentary adjective spontaneously. "You will learn after a while, my dear boy, that you are much happier with some one who cares a great deal for you than with some one who doesn't care at all."

"But whom——"

"I wouldn't say it." She turns quickly and calls Dolly. "I'll take the baby home. I think you had better stay away for a while."

Poor Reg turns and goes sadly up the fields, back to Edyth, to duty. As he comes out by the water gap he sees, loafing there, a figure which makes his fists ache. It is the dis-

reputable looking man whom Edyth has seen.
He looks at Reg, and then quickly turns in
the other direction, and starts walking, his
hands in his pockets, in the direction from
which Reg has just come.

Reg stops and half turns around, and then
sets his face.   He will *not* turn and look.

XVI.

R EG might have gone home happier had he
turned in time to see that Mary and little
Dolly went across the fields alone, with the
maid coming along behind, and the pail spill-
ing water and minnows at every step. It was
almost dinner time, and all the way home
Mary built up sentences of a cutting nature
to say to her husband. She felt sure he would
be there to meet her. She knew that she
would say nothing of the sort when she
actually met him, but it cooled her brain to
think she would.

She had never quarreled with Dick. Sometimes, when his indifferent air grew too indifferent, she had felt the storm rising; but
the sight of his calmness, of the light catching his blond head or the line of his perpen-
dicular profile, had always sent her back to
him happy again in the very fact of his being

there. Almost invariably silent, with no words to waste upon any one, Mary yet hung upon the very expressions of his face. She told herself that he only loved her because she loved him; she tormented herself with a thousand doubts, and then she thanked Heaven that he was so indifferent. He was hers.

This evening, as she drew near, she lost all memory of Reg and his poor little story in her delight at seeing Baylor again. It was a delight which time had no power to conquer. Mary's love was part of herself, the very spring of her nature, the incentive for almost every act of her life, remotely or nearly. But the slender, slow moving figure, with its eternal cigar, and hands idly thrust into pockets, was not pacing up and down before the door, nor reclining in the wicker chair under the trees. Seated stiffly on one of the hard settees which had disfigured the veranda for a generation, sat his elder half sister, Miss Baylor, looking hard and stiff and unflinching, as a woman usually looks when she has come to perform a duty. It was not easy for Miss Baylor to come here, and she ought to be honored for doing her duty as she saw it.

Careless Mary had never once thought of returning the visit that had been made to her. Richard had not suggested it, and she was not sufficiently accustomed to formal visits to think of it for herself. She came up now with her usual sweetness and grace and put out her hand. Her heart was sick with disappointment that her husband was not here, and her ears were alert for his step in the house.

"Come up, Dolly—my little daughter—and speak to your aunt;" but Miss Dolly held back. There was nothing in that face to please her.

Miss Baylor paid no sort of attention to her. "Where is Richard?" she asked dryly.

"He"—a set look came into Mary's face—"he went to call upon a friend."

"What friend?"

"An old friend whom he met the other day—a Mrs. Rogers, I believe," Mary said quietly.

A heavier gloom settled itself upon Miss Baylor's countenance.

"Nannie Vance! We all thought, at one time, that Richard and Nannie would make a match of it."

A quick flush went over Mrs. Baylor's face. "I suppose it would have been a great deal better if they had," she blurted out.

"Perhaps it would," said Miss Baylor unflinchingly. "The Baylors have been here a long time. Our great great grandfather was one of the earliest English settlers in Virginia, and there has never been anything but honor and respect for the family ever since——"

"Until now, I suppose." A temper is not a pretty thing in most people, but there is a damask rose tint on Mary's cheek that is lovely. Miss Baylor is not so severe that she cannot see it, and feel like muttering "A doll's face!"

"I do not consider it wise for a man ever to marry outside his own class, because people in different positions in life can hardly understand each other's customs." She cleared her rather raspy throat. "We can only do our best to keep up the honor of the family by offering advice, in whatever spirit it may be received."

"May I ask what I have done that is so different from the customs of your family?" There is anything but meekness in the tone of the inquiry.

"In the first place—and I do not see that it is necessary to go behind and beyond that—since you first attracted his attention and made his acquaintance, you have exercised all your power to keep Reginald Courtney at your side, and alienate him from the sweet young girl to whom he was engaged to be married. Whatever your motives may be I cannot say." Miss Baylor draws in her breath with the evident intention of going on, and then she sees a look in her young sister in law's face which is rather daunting.

"May I ask how I am supposed to know that Mr. Reginald Courtney is engaged to be married to any one, and what possible concern of mine it can be if he is engaged to fifty people? Or what possible concern of yours? I have been in the habit of choosing my friends

as they suited me personally, and I shall con-
tinue to do so indefinitely.   I am at a loss to
know whether you are sent by the young
man's mother or his sweetheart, to plead for
him, but you may take back my word that I
am entirely unacquainted with either, by their
own desire, and can hardly be considered responsible for my acts to people who do
not even exist—for me."

There was a slow red flush in Miss Baylor's
face.   "I come entirely upon my own account
—for the sake of the family name," she said.
There was spite and venom in the voice.   The
speaker's conscience would give her some
severe whips did it realize that she, a good
woman, whose daily work was mission schools
and benevolent visiting, was exulting in dealing a malicious blow.   There is a great art
in so educating our faculties that they may be
upon our own side in an argument.

"When your brother gave me that name he
made me its custodian, and himself my adviser,"
Mary said, her small head aloft ; and bowing
to her sister in law, she went into the house

and left her sitting there upon the stiff
wooden settee, to go home when it suited her
convenience.

Mary was miserable. She was ashamed and
mortified at her passage at arms with her sister
in law, and it seemed to her that she was surrounded and beset with trouble. She wanted
to put her hands over her ears and run. She
wondered what Dick would say; or rather, not
what he would say, but what he would think
and look when she told him, for of course she
would tell him all about it just as soon as he
entered the house.

She went slowly up the stairs, half listening
and looking back at every step for some sound
of her husband. She walked into the big, airy
bed room where she slept, and stepped into
the midst of a confusion of garments on chairs
and floor and bed. They were all belongings
of her husband.

A light came into her face and heart. He
must be at home. She went rapidly through
the rooms. He was not there; and then a
scrap of paper stuck in the frame of her mirror

caught her eye.   It was a hastily scribbled
note from Dick:

DEAR POLLY:
    I met some friends of mine starting for the mountains
for a four days' drive and trout fishing.   I have decided
to go along.   Kiss the baby for me.
Always yours,
R.

XVII.

NEXT door to Mrs. Ellery lived her bachelor brother in law, Dr. Charles Ellery, who might be called the doorkeeper of Ellenbro' life. He ushered in and out everybody of any consequence—anybody whose name, coming or going, was worthy of being announced. When Mrs. Ellery's husband died, long ago, everybody looked at everybody else, and, seeing futurity in the answering eye beam, looked the other way, and virtuously condemned the people who had no more respect for a sorrow than to prophesy its speedy consoling. But years had come and gone. Mrs. Ellery's crape had grown rusty, and had not been renewed. Dr. Charles and she were the best of friends, but there had never been a hinting of anything more. It may have been that Dr. Ellery had glanced enviously over the syringa hedge which divided the grounds

and sighed as he saw the comfort in the
widow's domain, but if it were so his sighs
had been lost on the air and had left no
echoes.

They were the best of friends. When
baking day came a napkin covered plate
always went through the hedge; and in the
autumn, when the bobwhite enticed the sportsman, and Dr. Charles went away over the
fields in his old brown corduroys, Mrs. Ellery
ordered no meat for her breakfast next day,
knowing that she would have broiled partridge
to give away.

Mrs. Ellery was particularly congenial to
Dr. Charles, inasmuch as she knew how to
hold her tongue. There were not many secrets
of Dr. Charles' keeping in whose holding he
asked anybody's assistance; but he liked to
know—as who does not?—that there was one
person to whom he could tell a story without
the certainty that names and dates would be
hunted out and the whole tale placarded on
the public mind. Then, too, there were counsel
and sympathy and womanly advice on the

other side of the syringa hedge; all of which
Dr. Charles appreciated.

It was Dr. Charles' custom on summer nights
to walk through the gate let into the hedge,
and to find his way over to the seats on the
grass, where Mrs. Ellery was ensconced for
evening coolness, fanning away gnats and
mosquitos with a big palm leaf fan. There he
would sit down with a sigh of content and
smoke his evening cigar. Dr. Charles was
slender and grizzled and bright eyed and given
to silences.

Tonight he has asked after the fall crops on
Mrs. Ellery's farm, and has heard her ideas
upon the silver question, as laid down by the
Baltimore *Sun*, and they have let the hours run
by, and darkness come on without a thought.

"Have you been up to see Baylor's wife
again?" the doctor asks. He is not particularly interested in Baylor's wife, but he has
gleaned enough of the current talk to know
that she is a popular topic of conversation.
He makes some concessions to Mrs. Ellery's
femininity.

His sister in law laughed a little uneasily. "I have not had the opportunity. Mrs. Baylor has not returned my visit."

"Did you want her to?" the doctor asks, the new light he is touching to his cigar lighting up some wrinkles at the corners of his eyes.

"Yes, I did," Mrs. Ellery says seriously. "I believe none of the idle tales they tell of her. She is young and thoughtless and pretty, and knows little of our ways. Sometimes, perhaps, our ways are a little countrified. But there is a good, true light in those eyes. She makes me think of a merry young girl. I can forget that she has a husband and a child. Possibly she forgets it too, sometimes, poor young thing."

"It isn't a good thing for a woman to forget. Any losses of memory of that sort are apt to be made up with something of a jog."

"Yes, I know, but I took a fancy to Dick's wife, and I wish she would let me be a friend to her."

"Is she unfriendly?"

"I have only met her once. Eliza was here this afternoon on her way there. I am afraid she was going to say something harsh to the poor young thing."

"She looks as though she could take care of herself," the doctor says.

"You cannot always tell. She has spirit. I like to see a woman with some spirit. Upon my word, Charles, I do believe that if she was one of our own girls, and did exactly as she does, there would be nothing said about her. The poor young thing isn't to be blamed for her up bringing. She couldn't help that."

The doctor rather likes to argue for the sake of bringing out Mrs. Ellery's palliating answers. "I don't believe one of our own girls would marry and then keep a young man dangling about all the time as she does. She had Reginald Courtney out in the meadow all the afternoon."

"Well, now—those may be her ways."

"How about his ways?"

"Who can blame a young man?"

Dr. Ellery laughs. "According to you,

there isn't anybody to be blamed, ever;" and
he rises to go home.

There is a sound on his gravel walk; and
then a sharp ring at his door bell, just across
the hedge.

"Who is there?" he calls.

The tall figure comes rapidly toward him.
It is Reginald Courtney. He finds his way
through the gate, slamming it back, and comes
quite near, as though he did not want to be
overheard.

"Hello, Reg," the doctor calls, while Mrs.
Ellery anxiously arises. "Anything the matter
at your house?"

"No." There is constraint in his heavy
voice. "But there is a friend of Mrs. Baylor
who is very ill—taken suddenly. I happened
to be there. The servants had gone, and Baylor—wasn't there. I offered to come for you."
Then, suddenly recollecting something, he
turned to Mrs. Ellery and then back to the
doctor. "She told me to speak to you
alone, and ask you to tell no one," he said
bluntly.

"Is it a man or a woman?"   There was the usual quietude in the doctor's voice; but Reg did not answer him.   He went back through the hedge and on into the dark road.

"Well, good night," the doctor said cheerfully to his sister in law, exactly as though he were going home and to bed.   "I believe it is going to rain before morning.   Better shut your windows;" and he followed Reg.

Reg walked on down the road, past the gates which led into the Baylor place, and which he had left such a little while ago.   Just beyond there was a little bridge which crossed Willow Pond.   There was a deep hole here where the stream had washed out an eddy for itself in the spring rains.

Reg stood here for an instant, looking over, and then he fumbled in his pocket and drew out a small object.   It was too dark to see it, but Reg knew what it was—a little red sea bean, which had been lying next his heart. He held it in his hand for an instant, and then he threw it over into the deepest part of the pool, and went on toward home.

The whole fabric of his life had changed and had taken on a rougher weave. There had come to him a sorrowful sense of the complexity of living. It had seemed such a simple thing all these years. There was only the daily coming up and going down of the sun, with enough work and play of the peaceful, commonplace order coming in between to keep life cheerful and sweet. And then suddenly everything had been changed.

Reg was a manly fellow. But he was young, and the experience of the world was not in him. Probably it never would be to any great extent. There are some natures which remain simple and primitive through everything, just as there are others which live upon fine and subtle distinctions, which are not well occupied except by analysis. Reg was one of the former. When Mrs. Baylor had come supplying some want which he had not known to be there, it had been like a new and wonderful gift, an outlook into a country of which he had never dreamed. He had been so overcome by the wonder of it all that it had intoxicated him. He had been blind to everything; he told himself he had been a fool.

He felt that the last few hours had put him through a great experience; that he was a man of the world, dead to the fresh inspirations of youth. Poor Reg! As well might a sportsman who had wounded a partridge talk of big game.

His conscience, too, came in and talked to him. "I have been a brute," he said to himself. He thought tenderly of Edyth, of her goodness, of her purity and sweetness, and— oh, man—of her devotion to himself. There was no room for a pang of jealousy here. He could rest in sweet security that his shrine would be his, and his alone.

He walked on and on until he turned in at his own gates. There was a cigar burning in the avenue walk, and as he drew nearer he saw his father walking up and down, his tall form bent, his arms behind his back. He stopped as Reg came striding on.

General Courtney is fond of quiet, as who that lives with Mrs. Courtney is not? Reg has never dreaded an interview with his father

in his life.   As he came up now, perhaps his
nerves were in a supersensitive state, but he
involuntarily braced himself for what he knew
had been awaiting him.

The old general put his hand upon his boy's
arm tenderly.   He could sometimes forget his
ancestors in the welfare of his descendant.
" Been out for a walk?" he asked pleasantly.

" I've been over to Dr. Ellery's," Reg said
doggedly.

" How is Charles?"

" Well, I reckon."

" Well, my boy—I am glad it was Charles
Ellery you were visiting.   It isn't often I have
any advice to give you, but——"

Reg shook himself.

" Don't grow impatient.   I know boys will
be boys, and there never was anything particularly straitlaced about me.   But there is a
certain sense of delicacy which you are losing
sight of in going about with this Mrs. Baylor.
Edyth is a young girl here under our care;
you are engaged to be married to her, and
you are not treating her with proper respect."

There was dead silence for a moment, and then General Courtney's hand rested a trifle more heavily upon his son's arm, and there was a little break in his voice, never a very determined one. "I want to have one son whom I can look upon without a reproach."

The family sorrow, the family skeleton which had been locked away so long ago that its bones had almost ceased to knock together with the sound which brings a shudder, was more potent to Reg just now than even his father could imagine. His conscience was sore, with the soreness of a conscience which has never been tried; with a soreness which was aggravated by a smarting pride. He had told himself that he was a fool, and here was his father fearing that he might go astray in the paths which had been marked all his life long by an awful warning.

He took his father's hand tenderly in his own. "You need not be afraid," he said. "I suppose I am a fool, but that is all over. I will go to Edyth and tell her so."

XVIII.

IT is a curious fact, and one which philosophers and Christian Scientists might put into their affirmative list of phenomena—providing that matter is entirely governed by minds—that when a man's inclination impels him, circumstances immediately fall into place and open a path toward his goal. There seems to be no other road to follow.

Reg had come home after his scene with Mary Baylor and eaten his dinner in a reproachful silence which his father tried to break by discussing why Virginia girls married so few titled men in comparison to New York girls.

"It seems as though they naturally would do so," speculated the general, "being, in so many cases, so nearly allied to noble old English houses. But it is true that in the North there are fewer chivalrous gentlemen for the young ladies to select from."

The little question of the average Virginia girl lacking one of the chief requisites to eligibility for a foreign marriage was entirely overlooked by the general.

Even this interesting subject brought out no responses—and the dessert of home made ice cream was eaten in a silence that corresponded with its own chill. After dinner Reg went out into the stables to smoke, and it was there that his eye lighted upon a bridle which he had borrowed from Baylor several days before, and had promised to return the next day.

It seemed imperative that that bridle should be returned to its owner; and then, he wondered if Mary was angry with him. If so—if she thought him an impertinent young scoundrel —he felt that he ought to go over and deny it —that he had not meant to say that he loved her. His cheek burned at the thought of her supposing that he meant to offer any disrespect. And she had laughed at him and sent him home! He would tell her that it was not necessary to be angry with him, not necessary for him to stay away ; that he was in no danger whatever.

That bridle must go home! He slung it over his arm, and went across the fields in the late summer dusk.

The house was all dark below as he approached it, except for a dim glow from the old lantern of painted glass which hung from the hall ceiling. He went confidently down the drive, expecting to find Baylor and his wife sitting there, his cigar aglow and her white gown showing in the rays from the lamp. But instead he heard rapid—almost excited—talk. He hesitated and half turned back. It couldn't be that Baylor and his wife were quarreling in their own front door!

There was a cry—Mary's voice in fright. Reg thought of the man he had seen that afternoon, and with hardly more than half a dozen steps he was upon the veranda and in the hall. Upon the old settee, where Miss Baylor had sat in judgment this afternoon, there half reclined a man. In an instant Reg recognized the shabby figure as the wreck he had seen that day. Mary was holding his head. Down the front of her white gown ran

a slender stream of blood. She held a handkerchief to the man's mouth. She drew her
breath when she saw Reg.

"Oh, come!" she cried, hardly knowing
what she said. "Lift him—bring him in. He
must not die here."

Almost mechanically Reg followed her
directions, lifting the emaciated figure in his
strong young arms, and carrying it to the bed
Mary had hastily prepared in one of the guest
chambers on the ground floor.

"Bring him here. Oh, lay him down easily,"
Mary said. "Poor boy!" There was a sob—
fear, sorrow, pity—all in her voice.

"Where is Mr. Baylor?" Reg asked.

"He is away." There was a straining
cough, and the man half rose on his elbow.
"Go! Go for the doctor, please, quick!"

Reg started, and then she looked up again.
"See Dr. Ellery alone. Speak to no one else,"
she said in an odd tone, looking at him as
though she had recognized him in that instant
for the first time.

XIX.

MRS. ELLERY had not finished fastening her windows against the prophesied rain, when there was a slapping of her knocker. She leaned out of an upper window, whose shutter she was pulling in. She recognized one of the Baylor servants.

"'S that you, Mis' Ellery?" he asked. "Th' doctor said as how I was to fetch you over to our house jus' as quick 's ever you could git thar. I'll wait down here, until you comes out."

"I'll be there directly;" and she put in her well ordered and unexcited head.

In five minutes she was walking down the road. She did not stop to question the man. She knew that she would learn nothing there. If he had had anything to tell it would have been poured out in a stream the instant she met him. He was silent with the dignity of ignorance.

There was a flutter in Mrs. Ellery's bosom,
although there was no apparent evidence of it
as she plodded along the dark country road.
There had been no real excitements in her
calm life for many years; those which had
come had been mostly echoes. Ellenbro's
scandals had been few, and the perpetrators
had usually been considerate enough to take
themselves away from the easily shocked vision
of their contemporaries, and let the tales of their
wrong doing come back unassisted by personal
corroboration, to be supported for a while by
malicious tongues, and then to be put away
in the minds devoted to the storing up of such
lumber.

The wide front door at the Baylors' was
standing open, with the settee against it, but
there was nobody in sight. The negro man
had left her at the gate and gone on to his
own little house in the rear. He knew his
wife must have been in the house by this time,
and this was the quickest way to learn the
news of the trouble.

Mrs. Ellery went on in alone, timidly.

There was a band of dim light which came through a doorway down the hall, and it was here that she stopped. The bed was opposite the door, and shaded from the light, but she could see a face surrounded by black hair lying against the piled up pillows, and hear a short, quick breath coming and going.

"Perhaps," she said to herself, "it is her brother." And then she remembered that Eliza Baylor had given her the letter to read, which had announced Richard Baylor's marriage, and he had said explicitly that his wife had no family whatever. But, here she was, sitting on the side of the bed, holding this man's hand, an expression of anguish upon her face.

The doctor stood by the old fashioned mahogany set of drawers, mixing some medicine in a glass. His sister in law walked over to him, and stood silent, watching the white powder dissolve under the spoon.

"I am giving him an opiate," he said composedly, as though everything had been explained. "He has just had a severe hemor-

rhage—and must sleep." And then he went
on with directions here and there, which Mrs.
Ellery began to follow out, trying to pay no
attention to that miserable figure which sat
there by the bed.

After he had administered his medicine,
lifting the man's head deftly and tenderly, Dr.
Ellery took his broad, old fashioned straw hat
from the chair where he had laid it, and started
out. Mrs. Ellery followed him.

"Where is Richard Baylor?" she asked.

"He doesn't seem to be here."

"Where is he?"

"I didn't ask. It might be embarrassing."

"Charles Ellery," his sister in law said,
with heat in her placid voice, "I am ashamed
of you;" and she went back without asking him
what she felt she must know—who the sick
man was. She went up to Mary, and put her
arms across the young woman's shoulders.

"Come away now, my dear. He is sleeping. The medicine is taking effect. I will
take care of him. You must lie down."

Mary let herself be led out into the hall.

There she sat down in one of the old leather chairs and began to weep, her shoulders convulsed with sobs, her head on the chair back.

Mrs. Ellery patted and stroked her hair. " There, there," she said. And then tenderly, " Where is your husband, my dear ? "

" I don't know." She puts her handkerchief to her mouth and chokes back her tears. " I am glad he is not here; but I wish he would come home. He wrote me a note saying he had gone to the mountains for three or four days—with some people I don't know."

" We must find out and send for him."

" No ! Oh, *no !* "

" Yes," Mrs. Ellery said; and then, still stroking her hair, " Who is the young man in the other room? He is very, very ill."

" Yes, I know, I know! It is all my fault. He told me that he was ill, and I did not ask him to come in. I let him die!" And her sobs began again, but there was no word as to who the stranger might be.

" He had no money," she went on. " I never thought of his having no money. He has been sleeping out of doors. I did not ask him to come here. How can I ever forgive myself?"

"You did not know." It was always Mrs. Ellery's way to comfort, whatever her thoughts might be. And her heart was heavy with fear. There was some secret, some unhappy story, which made this young woman fear even the husband she adored. "At any rate," thought Mrs. Ellery, "I am going to stay until Richard Baylor returns. I can do that much."

Suddenly Mary started up in a panic. "Dr. Ellery will tell no one that he is here?"

"No."

"He must not. I should have told him."

Mrs. Ellery went back into the bed room, her usually placid brows knitted. The sick man was stupid under the influence of the drug, as he lay there, his black hair dank, and his lips parted. She looked at him. Dissipation, illness, misery, were written in every line. What could this man be to Mary Baylor? After all, was it not wiser to let this strange woman, with her unknown ideas, go her own way? Why should any one come to champion her, when she must have in the background of her life stories they could never know? And then her youth, her prettiness, all came in to conquer. Mrs. Ellery turned the lamp wick lower, and settled into an easy chair with a sigh.

XX.

REG did not find Edyth that night. His new resolutions were so warm, and he had expressed his determination to his father so forcibly, that he felt as though his effervescence of virtue would not keep. He must get it over with at once. He even hesitated at Edyth's door as he went by, and almost made up his mind to knock, and call her out, to tell her that he had been a fool.

But the next morning he was glad that he had not done so. He had been thinking entirely of his own attitude toward himself, not of Edyth. He would have been putting himself into a sort of school of penitence for the rest of his days. What he could do was to go to her and tell her that he loved her more than any other woman in the world, and ask her to marry him at once. Morning found him still in the mind to do that.

It is a common custom in the South, since
the war, for servants to go home to their
own families at night. Very often they live
in a little house behind the "big house," but
oftener, in a town like Ellenbro', they have a
quarter of the town to themselves. The
houses, small and roughly made, are white-
washed, and sometimes very clean inside, with
treasures, presents which have been given from
time to time by "white folks," on mantel and
bureau. Zinnias and morning glories bloom
in the front yards, and except that the dancing
of other days is almost unknown, the social
life is much as it used to be in the "quarters"
of a big plantation. The people all gather
in the evenings and tell each other the news.

Cynthia, who had never grown to like Mrs.
Baylor, lived on the place, but she was a constant visitor to her friends and relations in the
town, and she retailed all the scraps of gossip
she could gather in the Baylor household.
She was a mulatto woman of more than ordinary intelligence and maliciousness, the result
of the vicious mixture of blood.

She had been visiting her friends this evening when Mary's strange visitor had come, but while she had gone too early for that knowledge to be part of her budget she told of the long afternoon which Mary had spent with Reg, and of Mr. Baylor coming in to find his wife out, and then hastily departing.

"I've been wonderin' all 'long jus' *when* he was goin' to leave her," Cynthia said contemptuously. "Anybody on this earth could see th' wasn' no quality 'bout her kind."

The next morning, as Mrs. Courtney's old black cook was going toward her kitchen, she passed the Baylors' gateway. Standing there in the fog of the early morning was Cynthia.

"Stop a minute, Aunt Sally," she said. "I want you to tell me if it's too early to gather mango melons."

Aunt Sally stopped and delivered her expert opinion upon this profound subject, and then Cynthia let out the story, which was more than she could keep.

"We've got company," she said with an evil smile.

"What you talkin' 'bout makin' mangoes fuh, when they's company?" Aunt Sally grumbled. "Mangoes ain' gwine to take no half 'n' half 'tention. When you make mangoes, you make 'em."

"I don' know how long he's goin' to stay. I don' know how long Mass Dick's goin' to be gone. You better let on to your young Mr. Reg that his nose is out o' joint."

"What you talkin' 'bout, gal?"

"Nothin' 't all! We've jes' got company. A gentleman's stayin' with us jes' now. Come late las' night. I ain' seen him yet. He 'pears to be feelin' porely."

An hour later, when Mrs. Courtney went into her kitchen to see that breakfast was going forward properly, she was told the story of Richard Baylor's departure, and that his wife was entertaining a gentleman in his absence. As she poured out the coffee at breakfast, she told it again.

Reg ate his bacon and eggs stolidly, paying no attention. He unconsciously waited, and his heart beats were a little slower, to see if

Edyth would make her additions to the tale, but he looked up and saw her gazing into her plate, her cheeks scarlet. Evidently she had not told his mother what she knew, and any further mention of the story was painful to her. Sometimes in this world it happens that people's impulses fit into their proper circumstances, and then, once in a lifetime, it comes about that two people are penitent at exactly the same moment, and are moved to say so.

After breakfast was over Reg hung about for an instant. Edyth took the flowers from the table and carried them into the sitting room, and he followed her. She had not looked at him at all. This last humiliation to Mrs. Baylor, this crowning proof of what she herself had said yesterday, had not made Edyth exult. She really and truly cared for Reg. She cared more that she should please him, and that she should have him for her own, than for anything else. Now that it looked as though he must see what sort of woman Mrs. Baylor was, there was an end to all resentment. She only felt sorry and disgusted that any of them had been mixed up with such a creature.

She trifled with the heavy roses and the sweet mignonette which her own hands had grown. And when Reg came and stood beside her, she trembled a little and nerved herself for her apology; but he spoke first.

"I want to beg your pardon, Edyth," he said, and some way the voice was one that the old light hearted Reg had never learned, "for what I said to you yesterday. It was unworthy of me. It would be a pity, indeed, if there was anything in the world that you could not say to me—the man you are to marry."

He put his hand out to touch hers. She turned and looked at him. There is in her face such honest love, tenderness, and womanliness, that she is pretty—and it is sure, and pure, and all for him! He puts his arms about her, and for the first time kisses her as a lover.

"I was wrong, too," she whispers in a minute. "I meant to tell you I was." Hers is the woman's heart—the sort which makes it possible for men to have wives.

Neither of them ever knew that much that was sweet in their lives had come through Mary Baylor—that there had been springs of feelings opened by the touch of her fingers, which would flow for each other through after years.

XXI.

THAT evening all Ellenbro' was ringing
with the story that Richard Baylor
had gone away, and that there was a man
who was very ill staying at his house, and
that Mrs. Ellery was there also. The last
fact was a later addition which was carefully
tacked on to the original tale by Dr. Charles
Ellery. "An old friend of the Baylors, who
had come in unexpectedly, very ill," he said.
"Mr. Baylor was away from home for a day
or two, and Mrs. Ellery, who was very fond of
Mrs. Baylor, had gone up to stay with her."

Somehow it seemed to change the look of
everything that Mrs. Ellery was there, and
very fond of Mrs. Baylor. "But for the Lord's
sake," said Dr. Charles to his sister in law,
" find out who this man is. I am afraid he is
going to die on our hands before Dick Baylor
gets back. I suppose, though "—there was a

whimsical streak in Dr. Ellery—"that the
earth would cover him from Dick Baylor. He
would be too indolent to even ask a question. I
have found out that he went off with John
Vance and some men from Baltimore to Rock-
away County, to fish. I sent Elisha after
him."

All this evening Mary has walked the floor,
feverishly, miserably. She looks out at the
trees about the house—the trees that were there
before she was born and will be there after she
is dead—and she hates them. She thinks of
the smell of the roses on the Twenty Third
Street stands in New York, and she draws in
her breath with a longing. If she were only
back there in the gay crowd, away from all
this trouble! She had never been nervous and
unhappy there. When Dick was gone, she
could picture him. He went out into a land
which was familiar to her, with people whom
she knew.

Here, it was all so different. She was strange
and alone, and she dreaded, for the first time
since she had known him, to see Dick come

back. Her heart was sick and frozen; she had lost her happy self confidence.

She moves restlessly and anxiously about her own room. Dolly has gone to sleep long ago, in the little room next to her mother's, which has been fitted up for her. There is hush and stillness and the shadow of death over the house—and disgrace, Mary thinks bitterly. What can she ever say to Dick?— and after all it is no fault of hers. She is in no way to blame; but—she shakes herself. It seems to her that she is being made to suffer for all sorts of things which are not her fault. She sees life as she has never seen it before, as something unlovely.

In a heart like Mary's all times of revolution are short and sharp. Yesterday—it seems so many yesterdays ago—she was happy. She despises herself, and everything else. Her husband no longer loves her—and this old shadow from away back in her girlhood has come up again to darken her life. She paces the floor, going up and down, up and down the long, bare bed room where so many Baylors

have lived their lives, where children have been
born and men have died. It all means nothing
to Mary. She has not the background which
traditions like these bring in an old family.
Happy go lucky Mary, who lives for the day
alone, whose blood is of quicksilver, going up
and down, has none of the pride, the feeling
which comes with ancestors and ancestral
walls, be they ever so humble.

Little Dolly stirs in her sleep and wakens,
sitting up. In one of Mary's rapid movements
by the door she sees her, a little dimpled,
sleepy eyed, rosy baby, sitting up in her little
bed, looking about at the room which she
hardly knew by night. Mary went to her, and
kneeling by the little bed drew the curly,
tousled little head against her bosom. "Oh,
my baby! My baby!" she said.

From down stairs there comes a hollow
cough. Mrs. Ellery has gone home for an
hour, and Dr. Ellery is sitting with his patient,
looking and wondering at the worn and cynical
face. The door opens softly and Mary comes
in, her face almost as pale as the white gown

which trails on the floor after her. She looks years older in this day and night. There are black rings about her sweet eyes, and the short hair, which usually curls so prettily and coquettishly about her forehead, is pushed back. In her arms she carries little Dolly, who looks about her amused and interested at the novelty of being taken out of bed at this hour and brought down stairs.

Mary walks straight up to the bed where her visitor lies, and puts the baby down beside him. "Here is the baby, Jack; you said you wanted to see her."

He puts out his thin, dark hand and touches the tiny, rosy, dimpled one which comes from the sleeve of Dolly's night gown.

"She looks like you," he said huskily. "She makes me think——" The poor thin face has been distorted by a smile which is almost like a grimace of pain, but even that glimmer goes, and Dr. Ellery, who is watching the scene from his seat by the window, sees two tears roll down the man's hollow and wasted cheeks.

"There never was a better woman lived on this earth than you are, Polly," the sick man said. "I don't know why all the sweetness and forgivingness should have been given to you, but I don't know any one else who has them." He spoke with labored breath.

"No! No!" she said. "It is only that I seem like that. I am only impulsive. Other women are good, and kind—better than I."

Mary's tears were on her cheeks. Dolly turned solemnly from one to the other. Dr. Ellery looked out of the window. He saw a man coming rapidly down the drive. There was no indolence in the walk now, none of that slow movement which belongs to a man whose leisure is hereditary and an integral part of his nature. It is certainly Richard Baylor, but it is a Richard Baylor whose every nerve is keyed up to the highest pitch, who walks down the drive with springing, rapid tread. He has only just left the train which is screaming its way across the meadows by the river.

Dolly is gazing into the strange man's face.

Too many things have happened to her in her little life, she is too prone—like her mother before her—to look into any new experience for its possibilities of pleasure instead of pain, to cry at the unknown. She has known many men, of all sorts, and that this visit has been the cause of taking her out of the bed which even at this early age she considers it a waste of time to inhabit, is nothing against him. She finds him strange, but not fearful.

She does not hear the firm sound of those footsteps on the gravel, coming up the veranda steps; but her mother does, and with a cry she flies out to meet her husband. Everything is forgotten in that first sound of his nearness, that footstep which has never failed to find its echo in her heart.

Baylor had been enjoying himself for a whole day. The attraction which Nannie Vance had had for him had been of the kind which could easily be transferred to her brother; and the men from Baltimore had happened to be of exactly his own sort. There had been stories told, and games of poker played, and the seek-

ing out of a camp. They had expected to
settle themselves for a week, but when Dr.
Ellery's man had put in his appearance with
the story that he was wanted at home, Baylor
had forgotten everything but his wife and
child and had started back.

When Mary came to meet him, when he saw
the dim light, his first thought was for Dolly.
"The child!" he said.

In that one expression Baylor told more than
he knew; and it was a knowledge that his
wife at once deplored and exulted in. "The
child" was not the distinct personality to him,
not the individual Dolly, but she was her
mother's child, the great bond between them.
She was *theirs*—and infinitely precious for that
reason.

Mary put her head against his shoulder, and
tears of relief, of self pity, ran down her
face. "Dolly is all right," she said. "But—
oh, Dick!"

"What is it? Tell me what it is?" There
was infinite tenderness in Baylor's voice. He
put his hand up behind her head, and held it

close to his cheek. "Can't you tell me what the trouble is?"

"I should have told you long ago, but—I thought it was all forgotten, all over, and there was no need of worrying you about it."

"Yes?" Baylor's brows were knit above the ruffled dark hair, but he held the slender figure of his wife close against his breast.

"Long ago—when I was a little girl, I had a sister Julia——"

There was a clearing up of Baylor's face. It took on again the look of calm. "But she died," he said with soft positiveness.

Mary lifted her head and looked up at him in wonder. "Did you know about her all the time?"

"Yes, my dear. Poncet told me when I first met you. I knew it was a painful subject, that she had died, and I did not wonder that you never spoke of her to me."

"But her husband——"

"Yes, and I know that her husband and she were unhappy—that he went out to get money for her in some way—anyhow—that he cheated at cards, and that he killed the man who caught his hand. There is no necessity of your telling me any of the story. I know it all. I knew it before I ever saw your face. Why should you have sent for me to tell me all this now? Did that tender conscience of yours begin to hurt? Or "—he laughed and held her tear stained face away from him and looked at it—"did you hunt about for an excuse to bring me home?"

"He—Jack—is here now. He wrote me a letter before we left New York. He wrote me another, and asked me to met him out by the spring—and I did. He is ill—he has no money—he is dying. Oh, Dick, sick and dying, he has been sleeping out of doors. He came again last night, and I took him in."

"What!" Baylor had said, as though her story was incredible; and then back into his old calm way, "You did perfectly right. Exactly as I should have wished you to do. Where is he?"

"There." She pointed to the bed room door.

Baylor put her away from him and walked back to the door, walked in, and closed it. He opened it again for an instant, and put Dolly into her mother's arms, tearing her delighted little hands from his face. " Put her to bed," he said. " You need sleep. I will stay here." Then back into the room he went, and held out his hand to the man lying there gazing at him with the big and brilliant eyes of one who might be gazing into another world.

" How do you do, Mason?" he said. "You ought to have come home before."

Dr. Ellery watched them with the eye of a spectator, until he heard Baylor's speech, and then he gave a violent start. It was probably the first time Dr. Ellery's nerves had ever so entirely controlled his movements in years. Starts are not common with a family physician. But in one moment he was himself again.

" It seems like old times to see you again, Dick," the man on the bed said, holding the cool, white hand in both of his hot ones.

Dr. Ellery came up and touched Baylor on

the shoulder. "Let me speak to you a moment," he said.

Baylor turned with him and they went outside the door.

"Would it not be well," Dr. Ellery asked in his dry voice, "for Mr. and Mrs. Courtney to be sent for? Mason cannot live through the night. The change is coming fast."

"You know him, then?"

"I have been the physician here in Ellenbro' for over thirty years."

"Then, Dr. Ellery, pardon me for saying that you have not done your duty in not attending to this before. You must have known that Mason Courtney was a dying man! My wife has no suspicion of his identity, or she would have done so. Death heals all breaches."

"Not with Mrs. Courtney."

"Yes, even with Mrs. Courtney. I never knew my own mother, but I have learned to know what the instinct is, in the mother of my child."

XXII.

MRS. ELLERY had gone home for an hour, to look about her house before coming back for the night. When she opened her gate she heard voices down by the big front door, and saw that it was open, and that two chairs had been brought down to the lawn and were occupied. There was a sound of tinkling spoons against the sides of glasses, and of low toned talk. Mrs. Courtney and Miss Baylor had come in to await their hostess, to get the particulars of the new development in the town topic.

They had been talking it over between themselves, but it was not so easy to take up in the placid presence of Mrs. Ellery.

"You see, we have been trying your raspberry shrub. Molly brought it out."

"Molly knows her mistress," Mrs. Ellery said comfortably, and sat down in a third

chair, as though she had nothing whatever
upon her mind.

"Where have you been all day?" Mrs.
Courtney asked pleasantly.

"I have been helping Charles with some of
his business."

"It is a very sickly season," Miss Baylor
remarked, and there was a silence.

"There isn't any use beating about the
bush," Mrs. Courtney said in her dictatorial
voice. "You may say that it is no affair of
mine, although I must feel differently, but it
is surely some concern of Eliza's that her
brother's wife is entertaining her friends in his
absence. Who is this man who is staying
there?"

"That I do not know," Mrs. Ellery says
positively. "I only know that he is an old friend
of Mrs. Baylor's, and that he is at death's door,
and that Richard has been sent for."

"There has been only one stranger in town,
and that was a most disreputable looking man,
something like an actor in appearance. Oh!"
—there is virtuous indignation in Mrs. Court-

ney's tones—"it is perfectly disgusting to have such a creature as that woman polluting the air of a town."

"She seems to me a very sweet and charitable woman, if she has taken in an old acquaintance who is dying."

"It is that man, then?"

"I did not say so."

"Well, here comes Charles; he will tell us." Mrs. Courtney is angry. Her hatred of Mary Baylor leads her beyond all bounds. "Charles, who is this man in Richard Baylor's house? We have tolerated enough from this woman, and it is our duty, as upholders of the dignity of Ellenbro' society, to know about her doings. She insulted Eliza only yesterday afternoon."

"Mrs. Courtney," Dr. Ellery said with his customary dignity, "your husband is waiting out here in my buggy to drive you home. I think he wants to see you very particularly. Perhaps he will tell you who the Baylors' guest is. He is an old friend of Richard's. Richard has just returned home."

There is that in Dr. Ellery's voice which silences Mrs. Courtney. "Is anything wrong at home?" she asks.

"I think your husband would like to see you at once. Will you allow me?" And with old fashioned courtesy he offers her his arm to walk to the gate.

The general sits with his head sunken in his collar. As his outline appears against the late evening sky, in the dusk, he looks old, old. He holds the reins with listless hands. Dr. Ellery puts Mrs. Courtney in beside him and they drive away. What they say to each other —how that heart broken old father tells of the wayward boy come home to die, taken in from the fields by a woman they have despised—is not for our ears.

It is a weeping and shaken woman whom Richard Baylor lifts down, and who goes in with his father to say good by to the boy she shut out from his home fifteen years ago. Reg is there too, very solemn and ill at ease, ready to fall at Mary Baylor's feet and ask her forgiveness. But the opportunity to do so is

not given him. The Baylors are up stairs,
alone, and Mary, drawing long breaths, after
her sobbing, is sitting nestled against her
husband's arm.

" I have been so unhappy here ! " she tells
him.

" It shall be no more," Richard Baylor says.
" It was all a mistake from the beginning.
We will go back now to our own life, and
Dolly shall be brought up in the world, not
in one little corner of it. The little flat is still
there in New York, and the theaters are open,
and everybody in town is back. We will
sell this old rat trap, and have money enough
to do as we like."

" Will you, Dick ? " she says, but she
says it wearily. She thinks of the dying
man down stairs; and then, too, there has
gone from Mary, in these weeks, some of
her youth. The purity of her joy in life
has been tainted. But she turns and kisses
him.

" It will be sweet not to think of other
people's ways. I never want Dolly to know

that there are any ways but the simple, natural ones."

"And be a Bohemian to the end of her days?"

"You can't be any more than happy," Mary says.

THE END.

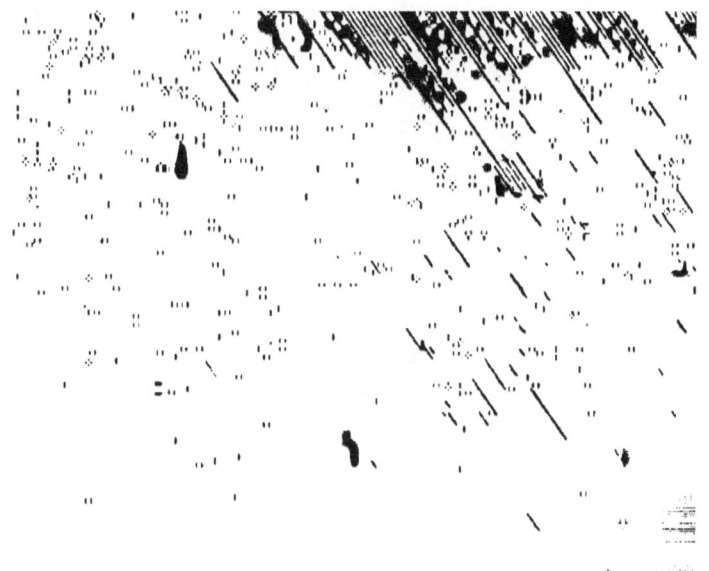

www.ingramcontent.com/pod-product-compliance
Lightning Source LLC
Chambersburg PA
CBHW031419020726
47499CB00005B/1498